The Lone Werewolf

by

Tim Forder

Published by
Melange Books, LLC
White Bear Lake, MN 55110
www.melange-books.com

ISBN: 978-1-61235-624-2 Print

Published in the United States of America.

Cover Art by Stephanie Flint

The Lone Werewolf
Tim Forder

A retired Union officer is given the gift of Skin-walker (Native American shape-shifter). Not long after learning about his abilities to shift into many animal forms, including a half-man, half-wolf form, a Lone Werewolf is forced to use his abilities against evil.

When General Custer's wife is kidnapped and held against her will within an impenetrable fortress, it's up to The Lone Werewolf to put his mystical magic to work to save her.

When the territory is terrorized by a tribe of Native American Vampires, it's up to The Lone Werewolf to take them on single-handed.

Is our new hero up to the task?

Author Note

This work of fiction has been heavily researched: The animals used in this tale have been researched, as have the myriad of historical personages that appear in this tale of western horror!

Chapter One
~ Somewhere in Texas, 1867 ~

It was sometime in the year 1867. The War of the States, or as some were calling it, the Civil War, had been over for about two years now.

I gave up my army career because of a bellyful of death. I had no plans of passing quietly as a Union Officer. Now I'd been roaming this great country, always heading westward with the idea of finding a new life for myself. I had no plans or ambitions except to see what was over the next horizon and leave my options open to whatever I may find over that next horizon. Not much of a plan, but it was working for me.

I occasionally took on the odd job to put a temporary roof over my head, to earn some money toward continuing my journeys, and when I got that restless itch, I'd see what was over the next horizon. In my journeying, I saddle trained some horses for a rancher who paid well for each horse I trained. I even sheriffed a small town for a spell, till the urge to move on got the better of me and I moved on. OK, I quit when I got the only deputy under me killed while we were trying to stop a robbery of our small bank that wasn't really worth robbing, let alone dying over!

When on the trail, loneliness was never a problem, except for the occasional want of a woman. Despite my upbringing I wasn't against scratching that itch with some small town fallen dove, and then moving on.

One night, somewhere in the great state of Texas, while enjoying some venison and a quiet camp, a cur wandered near the campfire and just stood there staring at me. Fighting off the temptation to go for my sidearm, I studied this pair of glowing eyes and a big dark area within the dark night. I guess since I hadn't made any threatening moves, it decided either to move in closer to my campfire, for the warmth or to get

1

Tim Forder

a better look at me, I couldn't say. As it neared the fire, I was able to get a better look at my quiet guest. It was a big brute; it looked like it had some wolf to it, but not totally.

I cut off a small piece of meat from over the fire and tossed it at the beast. The cur wolfed it down greedily. When it was finished, it went back to studying me.

I cut off a big piece and tossed it at the beast. The creature took its time with this bigger hunk of meat, apparently enjoying his gift. Moving slowly and making a point of appearing non-aggressive, I grabbed a second tin cup out of my saddlebags and poured some water into it from my canteen. Then I slowly walked to an area between the beast and where I had been sitting. The beast followed my every move with his glowing eyes. I sat the cup down and calmly went back to my place and went to cutting myself off another piece of dinner.

The cur looked at the tin cup, then at me, then back at the tin cup. He must have decided I was basically harmless. He walked over to the tin cup and greedily consumed the contents ... that's to say less the amount being splashed all around the tin cup, being greedily consumed by the dusty dry ground!

The cur then went back to his place, lay down, and looked to be settling in for the night. I did the same. The last thing I did was to ease my sidearm out of its holster and slide the pistol comfortably across my chest ... just in case.

The next morning, I awoke feeling fresh ... and alone. The cur was gone. I stood up and looked around, but all I could see was a beautiful landscape and my horse, which I named Horse, grazing on a grassy area that I picked out just for his pleasure. Thinking of the cur, I guess I was just nice to visit and a meal provider, and so it was back to the wild for my new buddy.

After taking care of my personal needs, I set forth stoking a new fire for some coffee. I was so busy at getting a fire going for my morning repast that I was suddenly surprised to discover I wasn't alone ... The cur was back; he was sitting about where I had put down his water cup the night before. I also noticed that he had brought me a rabbit for breakfast.

Seeing he had my attention, he dropped the rabbit and went back to his place by the fire, apparently patiently awaiting my preparation of his contribution to breakfast.

2

Not to be an ungrateful host, I sat to skin it and prepare it as the main course for our breakfast. After properly roasting the meat over the fire, I cut off a piece and tossed it to my new friend. I figured that if he supplied the main course, he should get the first piece. As he settled down to breakfast, I cut off some meat for myself and joined in. While we both enjoyed our rabbit meat, I finally spoke, "If you are going to stick with me, I'd better figure on giving you a name." While I gave the situation some additional thought, I tossed him another piece of meat. Eventually, full of his part of the rabbit, he just rested, staring at me ... perhaps waiting for his new name.

Problem: What did I know of naming dogs, wolves, or whatever this cur was? The closest I come to a dog was a puppy one of my men had found on a battlefield. He had named his new loving find "Pup" only to have a musket ball rip through his uniform coat, throwing 'Pup' into his chest, killing them both before he even hit the ground.

I couldn't very well name this one "Pup." No way was this big brute a puppy. I thought of naming him Dog, but what if I found out later that he wasn't a dog. I thought of naming him Wolf but, while he looked wolfish, I doubted he was all wolf. So what should I name him? I almost gave into the temptation to ask the cur what his name was ... I hadn't been out alone on the trail so long that I would expect an answer.

I said, still thinking it out, "I can't call you 'Big Brute'" ... I took his small growl as agreement.

I continued, thinking aloud, "You are a bit of a cur. How about I call you Cur?" His tail came up and wagged a little. I remember seeing the puppy doing the same when it was happy. "So you agree? Your name is Cur." The tail wagged harder, so forever he would be Cur. Unfortunately, just as the puppy wasn't Pup for long, this beast was destined not to be Cur for long.

We continued traveling together with the only difference being that he went to disappearing when we made camp. I kind of figured he'd gone back to getting his own meals while I went back to fixing just for myself. We continued traveling together for ... oh, I guess about two months. During that time if I came upon a town, Cur would stay holed up in the town stables with Horse. I'd just pay extra to the stable hand so he would feed Cur when he fed Horse. On such occasions I would, of course, occasionally look in on the two, making sure they were well treated. We did have trouble in one town. The stable hand was afraid of

Cur and would have nothing to do with him for no amount of extra money. So we left, me, Horse, and Cur. I did my resupplying at the next trading post I came across.

We had trouble there, too. The trading post was within fortifications and the Post Guard informed me the commander had rules against dogs on this post. I suggested Cur keep the Post Guard company for a few hours. He complied, to the enjoyment of the soldier who hadn't seen a dog since leaving his family's home. I resupplied and spent some time in the trading post's saloon enjoying a couple of drinks and a meal I didn't have to catch, kill, and prepare. Afterward, I was happy to find Cur where I left him, tail wagging at my reappearance outside the post.

We'd been back on the trail for nearly two to three weeks, just Cur, Horse and me, following my trip at the fort's trading post. We were enjoying a nice quiet nooner together when we heard a woman's scream.

Chapter Two
~ Trouble over the Hill ~

So much for a nice peaceful nooner.

Cur growled, jumping to his feet, while I ran to re-saddle Horse. Once done, I charged over a hill in the direction the scream had seemed to come from with Cur following close behind.

At the top of the hill, I halted Horse to spy out the danger and was surprised to find nothing. Nothing but open ground; nice, peaceful, open ground that would normally have demanded some time to look over and enjoy. The tranquility of the scene, including the peaceful sight of another hill, was interrupted when another scream sounded. I charged Horse up the next hill, and Cur followed without command as we raced forward together.

At the top of the hill, I found the source of the screams. An Indian squaw was pinned to a wagon wheel by two men in Confederate rags, while a third could be seen threatening her clothes and her decency with a large knife gleaming menacingly in the sun. Nearby, a fourth fellow who appeared to be enjoying something from a jug was totally taking pleasure in the improper antics of the previous three. All four men were having a fine time at the squaw's expense. I then took notice of a fifth man sitting off a little, on a log next to an old Indian. He had his gun on that old Indian, while also enjoying what was taking place at the squaw's expense.

I joined into the Civil War, not to fight slavery, but to get away from the boring life of farming chores. Blacks, Indians, they're all just humans to me, and that young lady was definitely not being treated very lady-like. While I would never consider marriage to an Indian woman, letting Confederate trash abuse one was not in my character.

In my observation and opinion, all this was too morally expensive for the squaw to let continue, but there were five of them and only one of me. I had fought worse odds while on horseback.

Not one to just rush into a battle, I moved Horse sideways, planting myself up next to a ridge that gave cover in its shade, while I planned my attack strategy. It would have been nice and easy to just sit and plug these ex-Confederate cutthroats with my Sharps rifle, but it would give someone in the group way too much time to kill the two Indians, thus making the Sharps not doable. I decided the course of action was a straight on attack, with my pair of Model 1861 Colt Navy revolvers blazing and Horse's reins in my mouth.

Leaning back, I easily found my extra Colt revolver that I kept in my left saddlebag, near the top for easy extraction when needed. I checked to make sure it was fully loaded with .38 cartages, minus one, and then removed my other Colt from its Union holster to make sure it was fully loaded, minus one. With the Colt Revolver hammer sitting directly on the firing chamber it was wise to have one chamber empty. If bumped just right or dropped with all six chambers full, the pistol could discharge a misbegotten round.

I removed two .38 cartridges from my holster's ammo pouch and loaded up the empty firing chambers of both Colts. With both pistols fully loaded, I'd have twelve shots for five targets. That's two rounds per target with two extra rounds in case I missed a target the first time around. I'm a good shot, but not perfect. Two extra rounds in truth might not even be enough. I was just going to have to pick my shots with some care and luck.

With a plan of attack, I kicked Horse into a gallop. As we charged the scene, I let loose two quick rounds of death from my left-hand Colt into the villain with the gun on the old Indian. He fell back with a blossoming red cloud exploding from his chest and the second round destroyed his face as he fell backward off the log he had used as his seat. The old Indian went backward with him.

I had heard no shot from the villain's piece and saw nether of my rounds had hit the old Indian. So what happened to make the old Indian fall back like he'd been shot? No time to worry about the old Indian right now.

With my right-hand Colt, I aimed for the ex-Confederate rage holding a knife over the Indian girl's clothes, but I held my shots as my target was obscured. The man tried to run, but Cur lunged at him, causing the two to go rolling out of sight and shot range. That villain was up to Cur, who attacked with gusto.

The two holding the Indian girl pinned to the wagon wheel had loosened their hold on her, causing her to drop to the ground. This was a bit of good luck, as it put her out of the line of fire and away from my next targets.

I took notice that they both were busy going for their side arms. Dropping the girl to the ground made my shots all the easier now that she was out of the line of fire. First, I plugged the one closest to me, with two shots destroying the chest area of his already ruined uniform. I quickly lined up on the second villain that had been holding the girl and let fly two rounds. One shot must have hit him in the shoulder, as he spun around. The second blossomed a rose of death from his back. Horse, being an experienced warhorse never once flinched from the small explosions of the Colts discharging their rounds of death close to his head.

As I targeted the last man, the one that had been enjoying a jug and overly enjoying the spectacle of the tormenting of the Indian girl, I discovered that he was now standing with pistol in hand and aiming down on me. While I let loose two rounds with my left-hand Colt, I took notice of his pistol bellowing out flames of its own. Just then, it felt like a tree hit me in the chest and then… blackness

* * * *

I must be in heaven. Only an angel could sing so sweetly.

I just laid there enjoying the beautiful melody. I didn't even think to open my eyes to take in the sights of heaven. I was so enthralled by the sounds. Then this putrid smell hit me like a right cross.

I sat bolt upright. "What the hell is that stink?"

Taking in my surroundings, I discovered I was inside a structure of long poles covered over with numerous skins sewn together. I have heard of such structures, but had never seen a tepee, let alone been in one. In the middle of the room was the Indian girl held earlier by those rags. While she stopped her singing, she didn't stop stirring something in a pot hanging over a small fire.

Looking my way, she spoke. "Stink you smell you. If can move, take soap and move to creek outside. Wash."

I was inclined to agree with her request, when I discovered I didn't have on a stitch of clothes under the bear rug into which I was currently snuggled.

"Cover self with bear skin, take soap. Leave. Live with stink for days. Not easy."

"Days? How many days? How is it I'm not dead?"

"Wash first, talk later."

I was reluctant, but I just had to ask. "How is Cur?"

"Your wolf?"

"You could say that …"

Her look answered before her words were out, but she answered anyway. "He give life in battle. Like bad one, he chose battle. Bad one knife him. He rip out bad one's throat. He shares honor of Grandfather's burial site."

She spoke in stronger tones. "Please, wash."

While my head spun with questions, I had to agree, I was really overpowering. I once scared up a skunk on my parent's farm, and I didn't smell this bad. Grabbing the bar of soap and holding the bearskin tightly around me, I made my way into the night. I was suddenly struck by the clearness of it. Even for a full moon, it was so bright. Everything was so incredibly clear. When I looked up, I was stunned to see it was a new moon night. No moonlight was unveiling itself to me. I don't know where the light was coming from because with no moon, there was no moonlight.

That wasn't all. Sounds from all around inundated me. I could hear life around me like never before. I heard the death squeal of a rabbit dying to become some predator's meal. I heard the distant scream of victory as a great predator bird flew off with his rabbit meal in his clutches. I heard the flap of a frog's tongue as it caught some meal on the fly. I heard the rattle of a rattlesnake and knew it was nowhere near! I could have stood there mesmerized by nature except I couldn't stand my stink.

As I approached the creek, I saw the fish swimming around. I also noticed from my reflection in the water that I must have been out for weeks. I had a bit of a scruffy mustache and beard. I don't grow either quickly. Normally I take days to grow a good 5 o'clock shadow. My brown hair was looking a bit longer than usual as well. Still stinking, I stopped inventorying my tall six-foot frame. I dropped the bearskin and, for modesty's sake, quickly jumped into the creek. The water was so cold I almost had a heart attack. To say the least, I made fast work of my creek bath—fast, but thorough. I couldn't get this stink off me fast enough. I was momentarily taken back by the smell of the animal fat content of the soap but, compared to how I stunk, there was no competition. I had to bathe, rough soap and all.

I was so intent on getting a thorough bath, I almost failed to hear the squaw approaching. When I did, out of reflex and modesty, I quickly turned my back to her.

"I'm not decent here."

"I here help with back. Use ointment on back where bullet hit. Hand me soap."

"So you nursed me back from death's door?" I handed over the soap.

"Grandfather's say use magic ointment gives you second life."

Remembering the sight of the old Indian falling from my shot of the renegade next to him, I feared I had failed to save his life. "So the old one, your Grandfather, did not survive the attack and my rescue attempt?"

"He live. We go Native lands. He want be buried. Gray coats attack. He very old. His time near. He hope die native land, in Navajo Territory. It not be."

After a pause, while doing a good thorough washing of my back she continued. "After attack, he know he not make journey to native grounds. He knew you not survive trip even with ointment. He say bury him here. Treat you with magic ointment he plan buried with him. Ointment be buried to keep from evil ones. Bravery for two Indians proved ointment destined for you."

"So I gather it was this ointment that had me stinking like the dead? What is this ointment you speak of?"

"Better stink like dead, than be dead. Finish bath. We talk, eat hot dinner, make feel better." With that, she left as swiftly and as quietly as she had arrived, just like the calm night wind.

Even though I was getting used to the creek coldness, I quickly finished my bath and, for modesty's sake, donned the bearskin and made my way back. Outside the entrance of the tepee, I found my saddlebags. I pulled out my spare clothes, but could not find my boots, holster-rig, or hat. I moved away from the tepee into the concealing darkness of the night and got dressed. I really was not going to feel normal until I had my holster-rig with my trusty Colt revolver. My war years left me not feeling dressed until I was armed to kill.

Upon entering the tepee, my Indian savior pointed to my hat, boots, and holster-rig, all lying on what had been nearly my deathbed. I put on my boots and then my holster-rig, careful to remove my Colt and check its readiness. To my surprise, I found it had been reloaded. When I picked up my hat, I found my second Colt lying beneath it. Checking it, I found it had been reloaded as well. I noticed each was reloaded by a novice who did not know what they were doing. Both pistols were fully loaded with their hammers on live rounds. I removed one round from both pistols and made sure the hammer now rested on empty firing chambers. After all, these pistols were not Remington pistols, which someone told me had solved the problem of the hammer and could be kept fully loaded at all times.

"Grandfather say reload weapons. Now sit, eat." She ordered, holding out a wooden bowl that not only smelled great, but also had my stomach growling again.

"Sit, eat, before stomach scare off animals here."

I gladly did as I was told. "You're Navajo. How is it you're here in Texas?"

While she answered my question, it gave me time to see her. In the firelight, she reminded me of my now dead sister: tall and slim like my sister, and even though her hair was dark like a raven's wing and my sis's hair was a light brown, they both wore their hair similarly with bangs in front and the rest of the hair pulled back. I took note that she was wearing a buckskin tunic, pants, and moccasins.

She got even more serious than usual, if that was possible. "Have you heard of 'long walk' or what my people called 'Hwéeldi'?"

"Afraid not."

"Not be afraid, you not Navajo. Great White Father in Washington say reservation better for Indian. Not Navajo lands. Navajo lands feed us, clothe us. Indian leaders disagree with Great White Father. Blue coats starve us. Say choose leave land or starve in winter. Navajo leaders agree move. Blue coats march us many, many miles to reservation in south New Mexico. Some, like father, not want blue coats be chief and escape 'long walk.' Father, Grandfather, and I escape one night. My father stole three blue coat horses. Horses heard, shots fired, father hurt. By morning, we stop, camp. Father die from blue coat ball. We bury father. Go. Blue coats not follow. Make camp later. Grandfather teach live off land. We fine. Grandfather say time we go native land for final rest."

With dinner cleaned up, she continued. "First, Grandfather …"

"One minute, please." I put my hand up. It was past time to ask. "What of my horse?"

"Horse in a corral with horses of bad ones. Saddle and bad ones' saddles, near corral."

"What of … the bad ones?"

"I check dead bad ones for things useful. Then roll to ditch what have no bottom. Easier move camp from dead, but you not survive move. Move dead. Weapons and few coins next your saddlebags outside, clothes, useless rags. You check later.

"You live. Grandfather's magic ointment handed from Medicine man father to Medicine man son. Grandfather refuse use ointment and refuse pass ointment to his son, father …"

"Mind if I ask why?" I interrupted.

"Magic ointment use for great good or great evil. Magic ointment give great power. Great power bring great temptations to evil. Grandfather not trust self with ointment and not trust son's warlike. Grandfather take ointment to grave, keep from evil ones. Then attacked.

"Old Indian and squaw no match for five bad ones with weapons. Then you came. Risk life for two Indians. Fought to death. Grandfather believe you die without ointment. Grandfather believe you warrior with great and powerful spirit. Grandfather order me use ointment, save your life."

"Good, evil: I don't understand." I felt the need to interrupt, getting overwhelmed with all this information.

"Magic ointment give one great spirit powers of nature. Magic ointment has great healing. Grandfather instruct use ointment on body, then over injuries. Help heal."

Reflexively, I pawed my chest where I still remember getting pole-locked twice before nothingness set in.

"You shot twice: One shot smashed bone right arm and leave out your back. Second shot hit in side. Smash three ribs, stop there. I remove bullet."

From her description, I'm guessing .40 to .50 cal shoots. Amazing

I'm still alive. I couldn't help but test the movement of my right arm, which moved flawlessly, as if rude intrusion of lead never happened.

"Magic ointment save life."

"OK, magic ointment save my life with your help." I almost got a reaction from that. So I grasped that the ointment that stunk so bad revived me rather miraculously. "So what is this powers of nature stuff? What did you mean 'gives one great spirit powers of nature'?"

"Better you see." She grabbed an animal pelt from a skin bag she had lying next to her. I hadn't previously noticed it because the animal hide bag was hidden from the fire light.

"Must do what I say: Leave tent, take off clothes. Put belt around body, tie rawhide strips around you, then think great wolf."

The slightest sign of a grin, and I would have expected some joke, but she was completely serious. I reluctantly took the pelt belt from her and did as instructed. Once outside the tent, I walked over to the wagon. I then hesitated. Whether out of modesty of having to remove my clothes or the absurdity of her instructions, I couldn't say.

I looked around awhile still amazed at how and what I was seeing; I had never seen in the dark so well. It seemed totally crazy, but that Indian woman had saved my life. I'd seen enough death during the war to know for all intents and purposes, I should be dead, and I wasn't. On that note, I started shedding my clothes. I did so while keeping an eye on the tepee entrance, but saw no movement from within.

After removing all my clothes and placing them on the wagon for easier retrieval later, I quickly put the animal pelt, which did appear to possibly be wolf hide, around me, tying the rawhide straps tightly around me and pictured a wolf in my mind.

Chapter Three
~ The Werewolf ~

A force pulled me onto all fours, followed by an enticement to run free to which I yielded. I made a point of running in a direction away from the corral to avoid startling Horse and the other horses. I ran up to the creek and looked into the water.

I jumped back at the sight of a grey wolf as big as I had ever seen. At first, I doubted I could be looking at myself. Experimentally, I pawed my image. After watching my wolf self shimmer in the ripples, I took interest in my wet paw. There was no doubting it. The big Grey Wolf was me.

Giving in to my glee, I howled in delight and was answered. First, I heard from a corral of scared horses, Horse being one of them, and then I heard an answering howl.

For the sake of Horse and the others, I ran some distance in the direction of the answering howl and howled again. Again, my howl was answered. I moved in the direction of the answering howl.

I howled once more, and again I was answered. I can't say how, but I knew it was a female who answered me. I ran toward her to find out.

As I ran, I savored the feel of the wind rushing past my muzzle, my ears, and my lean furry body. I was a four-legged artillery ball rushing to my destiny. I couldn't say how far or even how long I rushed over the rough, dry terrain, but just as I turned a rocky corner, there she was. She was beautiful. Her grey coat was so light in color, she almost looked white.

I could have stood there gazing into her beautiful, thoughtful eyes all night, except a low growl informed me that we were not alone. I turned my head to discover about five more wolves, a mixture of male

13

and female, with a big, ugly male standing in front and apart from the rest. He was the dominate male and pack leader.

His low, menacing growl matched his stare and his posture. Everything about him said, 'She's mine. Leave or fight.'

I looked him over: he was bigger and badder looking than the rest of the males, but he wasn't even half my size. I could take him easily. I could have this lovely female for myself and become leader of the pack all in one. Hell, as leader of the pack, I could have all the females.

I started to match his stance, ready to fight this ugly cur for the love of the pale-furred beauty. I was going to fight for the right to have this bitch, and for her right to have my puppies. Cody O'Conner never ran from a fight. Even outnumbered by the grey coats, Cody O'Conner never backed down from a fight. Cody O'Conner never walked off a field of battle anything but victorious.

Cody O'Conner was a man in wolf's skin. What the hell was I doing? I turned and ran off, not even daring to look back. That beautiful bitch wasn't mine and never would be. I was a fraud, a cheat, an interloper, a phony wolf; I was still a man.

I ran with the gnawing image of that beautiful bitch clouding my mind, filling my every thought.

Eventually, I just started enjoying the feeling of the wind in my fur while getting that gorgeous bitch out of my head and out of my life. Then I caught it, a whiff of venison. Deer. Dinner.

I pulled up short and sniffed the air. Yes. There was a deer herd nearby, dinner on the hoof. As fate would have it, I was downwind of them. They didn't even know I was around.

I didn't want to make my job harder by scaring off my dinner and having them take flight too soon. I eased closer, crouching behind any scant cover I could find, and, soon, there they were. It was a fine herd, too numerous to count, and I didn't need to count them. I just needed to bring down one, and dinner was served.

As I neared them, one must have sensed or heard something of my approach. With a bark from that one, they all popped up their heads as one, and the herd started moving, tentatively at first, but definitely away from the danger. Away from me. My dinner was going to be difficult, but still near at hand or paw.

I moved in closer and the herd ran. They ran for their lives, and I was right on their tails. I was keeping pace with them while picking a target, picking out one slower than the rest. There he was, bad hind leg and all. I charged, and the herd dashed for their lives, leaving one behind them. My dinner. I ran up to the buck, smelling his fear. He dodged away, and I moved with him, looking for a chance to grab him by the throat and bring him down to kill.

The buck kept dodging me. As it tired, I finally saw my chance and lunged for its neck, but before I got a good hold, it tossed me off. The chase was afoot. I kept feinting at its throat, and it kept evading me, but I could feel it growing exhausted. Eventually, I saw my chance, lunged for the buck's throat, got a good lock, and brought it down. I ravaged the throat, killing the buck.

I started to have my dinner, when I remembered the squaw and my humanity. I dragged the dead buck back to camp. On nearing the camp, I heard the horses in the corral moving nervously at the smell of death and of a predator.

I made a point of approaching the camp from the side opposite the corral, keeping the tepee between the corral and me. I found my squaw waiting for me by the tepee entrance. She was pointing to my clothes. I got the point and, dropping the venison at her feet, I bounded off to get dressed.

I pawed at my stomach, picturing myself, my human self, and the rawhide that both was and wasn't there came untied. As a man, I got up off all fours and quickly, for modesty sake, pulled on my clothes as the sun started rising. I was both tired and exuberant from my night's adventure. I even discovered a pang of sorrow over what might have been with that beautiful bitch I left behind.

On entering the tepee, my squaw just ordered, pointing at the bedding, "Sleep now, talk later."

I couldn't argue with that, but as I lay down, I felt so charged with possibilities I didn't understand, that I doubted I would sleep.

Chapter Four
~ The Great Grizzly Bear ~

Hours later, I awoke, ravenous. Sitting up, I gladly noticed my teaching squaw again at the stew pot, fixing my venison for me; I could tell from the delightful smell wafting throughout the tepee. I knew she was fixing this meal for me, as I had learned that this squaw was a vegetarian. My teaching squaw, seeing me awake, continued with my education.

"You learn fast. First night in the wild, bring back a kill," she said, while looking to her cooking.

"Mind telling me your name?" I said, interrupting the quiet.

"Me Abedabum," she answered.

That was a mouthful. I strongly doubted I'd ever get that right. I remembered how some Indian scouts employed to assist the army were given English translations of their Indian names to communicate better between Indian scouts and the troops.

"Is there an English translation of your name?"

"Means dawn or morning light," she answered.

"How about I call you 'Dawn'?"

She nodded her approval. "I call you 'Captain Cody O'Conner, United States Calvary, Retired'."

"Just call me Cody," I replied, and almost added, 'Where did you get my name from?' Almost. The 'retired' answered the unasked question. It was from discharge papers I still carried in my wallet. "Now that I just experienced the spirit of nature, can you please tell me what I experienced? What happened to me?"

"You, Captain Cody, now Skin-walker."

"What the hell is a Skin-walker?" I didn't bother to correct Captain

Cody.

"Not hell, your gift as Skin-walker from Great Spirit. Ointment and special animal pelts allow change to many great, powerful animals. Take off pelt and change to human."

"Sorry, I meant no disrespect, but all this is hard to take even after experiencing it."

"Gift from Great Spirit can be great evil. Most Skin-walkers witches. Broke taboos and killed to gain gift from Great Evil One. Do evil for Great Evil One. My people fear Skin-walkers. Keep gift secret. Skin-walkers hard to hurt, hard to kill, but not immortal."

"Grandfather know temptation of power of gift. He no use gift, feared not strong to fight temptation. Grandfather not pass gift to son: Father good man. Grandfather fear not able to fight temptation. Grandfather plan bury gift. Prevent use by evil ones. Grandfather believe you great warrior with strong spirit for good. Grandfather instruct save your life with ointment. Grandfather tell me teach you. Now time you learn by doing."

She reached into the bag that the wolf pelt came from and handed me a different pelt. Like the wolf pelt, I did not recognize the new pelt. "Go out, take off clothes, put on pelt like first pelt, and think of great powerful grizzly bear."

I did as instructed and changed out of human clothes and into the pelt belt, and suddenly noticed I could see farther, and I was standing taller. Remembering how I got a great look at my gray wolf self in the creek reflection, I returned to the creek to look at the new me, the great grizzly bear. My first response was to jump back from my closeness to such a fearsome looking beast. My second response was to verify what I was seeing by touching my reflection and seeing myself touch my grizzly bear reflection. Looking beyond my reflection, I caught the motion of fish and my grizzly mind said food. I got hungry and went fishing. I fell down to my four paws, lumbered into the creek, and momentarily froze at the sight of a great large bear looking back at me. After recovering from my own image, I got to fishing.

Finding the fish too small to bother with, I remembered the deer and went lumbering off in search of more venison. I was having a ball lumbering around, standing my full height and seeing how far I could see, when I smelled smoke. My instincts told me to run in the opposite direction, but my humanity won out, and I went lumbering off in the direction of the smoke. As the smell grew stronger, I could see the fiery glow in the distance and was tempted to head in the opposite direction once more, but again my humanity won out, and I traveled toward the orange glow of destruction.

As I got closer, I heard a woman screaming and the sounds of struggling, mixed with manly laughter. My bear self said, 'This is not your concern. Let's go find something nice and tasty to eat.' My humanity said, 'Someone is in danger and it sounds like a woman. Go help her.'

My humanity won out once more.

So I lumbered in the direction of sure danger, and on breaking into the clearing, I discovered a large wagon fully engulfed in flame, the contents of which was strewn about, some of which was also creating little fires here and there. My bear mind said, 'Fire. Run away.' Then my bear mind got interested in what lay around and what I could eat. My humanity said something is very wrong, investigate.

Some distance ahead of me, clearly in view by the firelight, were two men and a woman. One man was holding the woman's upper body down while the other man was wrestling, and laughing, from between the woman's struggling legs. When I heard the rending of cloth and the woman screaming again, I stood as tall as possible and let out a great roaring growl that froze the men in their foolery until they discovered the source of the interruption.

When they saw me, they started falling all over themselves trying to get more space between them and me.

One screamed, "Bear!"

The other called out, "Where the hell did he come from?" Both forgot all about the woman, drew their side arms, and let the lead fly. Most of the shots zinged by like angry mosquitoes in a hurry to get gone. A couple hit me, but I hardly felt them. I strongly doubted the shots were doing me any harm, but out of anger, I let out another bellow of rage, and the two started a running.

One yelled, "What about the woman?"

The other yelled back, "The hell with the woman. That bear can have her. I'm getting out of here." The two ran off lickety-split.

After they disappeared, I heard horses rushing off. I lumbered over to the woman who appeared dead. Getting my muzzle close to her face, I could just make out her breathing. I quickly rushed back to Dawn's encampment. I doubted I could help her anymore in bear form.

When I reaching camp, I quickly changed back to my human form and even before I was totally dressed, I yelled out, "Dawn, come quick."

She must have heard the urgency in my voice, because she was at my side in a pistol shot.

"Get Horse and two other horses saddled fast. I'll meet you by the corral in a minute." Without questioning, she did as I commanded. After getting fully dressed, I rushed into the tepee and grabbed my hat, because under it was my holster rig. I then grabbed up my rig, and after donning it, pulled my trusty Colt and made sure it was fully loaded minus one. Earlier, I had seen to it that my second Colt was placed in my saddlebags. I quickly found my saddlebag and removed the second Colt. After checking to make sure it was fully loaded minus one, I placed it inside my tunic. Now, dressed and armed, I rushed out in the direction of the makeshift corral.

Dawn was just saddling the third and last horse. I quickly jumped onto Horse's saddle, and, Dawn followed suit, jumping into a saddle of one of the dead Confederate's horses.

"Let's hurry, a woman's life may be at stake."

We headed in the general direction I had come from in bear form. I looked back pleased to see that Dawn apparently knew her way around on a horse, as she was keeping up with me while leading the third horse behind her.

In bear form, I had made quick note of some trail markers to use to get back to the fallen woman's aid. I was finding the markers easily. Before I knew it, I was back to the clearing. All the little fires where just smoldering out, and the covered wagon, the big fire, was just about out. I had figured on this, so I never did figure to use the fire's flames to find my way back to the victimized woman.

I rode straight up to where I had left the woman and dismounted before Horse had entirely stopped. The woman was still there, lying like a child's discarded toy doll. I was checking for a pulse as Dawn ran up and moved me away so she could properly examine the woman.

"Get fire going so I better see woman's injuries," she ordered.

That wasn't difficult. I tossed some wooden trash into the remnants of a campfire and grabbed a piece of wood, the end of which was still burning from the covered wagon, and tossed it into the campfire. I walked back to see the woman, her head resting in Dawn's lap.

"She fine," Dawn said. "Last thing she know fear of large bear." The last almost sounded accusatory.

"I'm Captain Cody O'Conner, Union Calvary, Retired," I said, kneeling down toward the two. I figured adding the rank might help add authority to the situation and might be a comfort to the woman. "Can you tell me what happened here?"

"My husband and I..." She suddenly started crying. "They killed my husband."

Then she settled down again. "Sorry ... my husband, Dr. Adams, and I were part of a wagon train moving west toward California. While camping for the night, the wagon master, two of his men, and two strangers approached our night camp. The wagon master told us the two strangers were looking for a doctor. The strangers said Indians attacked their mining camp and four of their friends were injured badly. Word was that the wagon train had a doctor with them. The men begged my husband to leave the wagon train to help the injured men. The two promised to return us back to the wagon train in four days. The wagon master strongly warned against it. My husband felt it was his duty to help those injured. Come morning, we pulled our wagon from the train and followed the two. They said we would make camp for the night and travel to the mine camp the following mid-day."

She paused, seeming to have to think about what happened next. "We made camp. I made dinner for all. ... The two said I had made a very nice dinner. They said ... I would make an even nicer dessert and laughed ... I didn't get the joke, but my husband seemed to ... and ordered them to keep a civil tongue if they expected him to work on the injured ... They laughed even harder and both took out their guns and shot my husband."

Dawn gave me a look that clearly asked if I had found her husband. I just gave a little nod in the affirmative and hoped my grim look answered the rest. I had found the charred skeletal remains among the ruins of the covered wagon. It appeared to me that they had dumped his dead body in the wagon and set it ablaze. At least I hope Dr. Adams was dead at the time.

A horrid look of remembrance came over her face. "They just shot my husband ... and laughed. They then..." She passed out.

"Dawn, think she's going to be all right?"

"She need real medicine man soon. Their fort not two, three days from here. Grandfather say he plan to skip fort, go around it. He say Indians not welcome in fort."

"Know anything of this fort?"

"Fort Union. Before your War of States, was big trading post. Became Blue Coats fort in war. After war, fort keep Indians way blue coats want. Indians not welcome."

"You're with me. You'll be welcomed if I have to bang some heads together," I said in my best commander's voice of authority.

"Hmmm," she replied.

"It'll be light soon. Can you find your way back to camp?" She just gave me her single nod in answer.

"Pitch camp and come back here with the wagon and spare horses. I'll stay here and see to Mrs. Adams and watch over her."

"If evil men come back?"

"I should be so lucky," I answered venomously. I would just love to get my hands on those two sick bastards.

Thus said, we both made for where we left our horses. Dawn went over and untied the horse she had come on. Horse, even though I had not tied him down, was just where I left him in my haste to get to the injured woman's side. I removed my .44 cal. Henry repeating rifle from its scabbard, leaving the Sharps in its separate rifle scabbard. If the men returned, they most likely would not be alone. I figured the Henry rifle with its 16 shots per load and its ability to shoot 28 rounds a minute would serve me better than the Sharps, which was best used for sharpshooting or sniping from a long distance.

I was checking the loads on the Henry as Dawn rode off, leaving a dust tail behind her. I heard Indians where good on horseback. I didn't know it included their women folk as well.

With the sun coming up, it would be hot soon. With my rifle in hand, I found some wood and a good piece of wagon cloth that had escaped burning and made a lean-to over Mrs. Adams. The day went by quietly. My nooner consisted of hot coffee and beef jerky from my saddlebag. I persuaded Mrs. Adams to drink some water a couple of times, but for the most part, she just lay quietly under her lean-to.

It was near time for the setting of the sun when Dawn returned. One of the Confederate horses pulled the wagon with the other horses tied behind the wagon.

While Dawn went about getting the dinner fire ready and preparing dinner, I carried Mrs. Adams to the wagon. I made her comfortable for the night and saw to the care of the horses, as well as my own Horse.

We had a hushed dinner, after which we laid out our bedrolls and laid down to get some sleep. I made a point of having my rifle, cocked with hammer back, at my side in case of a midnight intruder, especially the two-legged kind.

After an uneventful night, we ate a quick breakfast and hit the trail, with Horse and I in the lead and Dawn following with the wagon.

Chapter Five
~ Somewhere in New Mexico ~

The trip to the fort took three days, during which time Mrs. Adams was conscious only for a bit. She mostly rode calmly in the back of the wagon, sliding in and out of consciousness. She occasionally took some water. On the second day, she even took some vegetables from a meal Dawn had mashed up especially for her. During the time Mrs. Adams was with us, nothing was said of skin walking or of my continual education.

We arrived outside of a fort that looked like it had clay walls around noon. A rifle-armed soldier stepped forward, disrupting our progress.

"State your business."

I had to stop or Horse would have run him over. I chose to give Horse a breather. "I am Captain Cody O'Conner, Calvary, Retired," I said, in my best commanding voice. "I have a woman in the back of the wagon in bad need of a doctor."

"Let them through," the guard ordered.

We entered the area of clay huts and tents we had seen in the distance and another soldier stopped us. I spoke before he could order us to stop. "Where is your commanding officer, and where can we find a doctor for a badly injured woman? Mrs. Adams, in the back of that wagon, is in serious need of a doctor."

"The Commander can be found in the large building straight ahead and to the right. The hospital is straight back and a little to the left."

Turning in my saddle to better face Dawn, I ordered, "Take her to the hospital, while I see the commanding officer."

The soldier interrupted. "But she's an Indian ..."

"There is a very sick woman in the back of this wagon. Is there a

23

problem … soldier?" I said in my best dominant commanding officer voice.

"I guess not, Sir."

"YOU WHAT, SOLDIER?"

"NO SIR, SIR," he snapped back, fearing he'd gotten his boot stuck in his mouth and might spend the next few months cleaning out the horse stalls.

"Soldier, go with them and make sure there are no problems … UNDERSTAND?"

"Yes sir, Sir." The soldier snapped in his best military form.

As the soldier mounted the wagon seat, with, "Pardon me, ma'am," to Dawn, the Indian squaw, I dismounted Horse, throwing his reins over the horse rail. I entered the earthen building. Marching up to the officer behind the desk, I demanded, "Who is in command?"

Assuming I had rank, the soldier stood, saluted and answered. "Colonel Christopher 'Kit' Carson, Sir."

"Please inform Colonel Christopher 'Kit' Carson that Captain Cody O'Conner, Second Regimental Cavalry, Kansas City, Retired, is here to see him. It pertains to some ex-Confederate rags and a woman I found on the trail in very bad need of medical attention."

The soldier quickly went to the closed door, knocked, and entered. Soon, he reappeared, making a point of holding the door open for me to enter.

A very impressive gentleman with hair and a mustache that had a proper military point asked, "So, how is Mrs. Adams?"

The fact that he already knew her name caught me by surprise. It must have shown.

"A wagon train came through days ago. The wagon master was concerned over a wagon that left his train prematurely with a Dr. Adams and wife. He made it clear that they left his train against his wishes. He then tried to order me to send troops out looking for them. I assume you just brought in Mrs. Adams for our doctors to treat?"

"Yes, sir. Found Mrs. Adams about two days east of here." I told her tale. "She claims the men were interrupted by a large bear. If the bear is not an illusion from fright, I can only guess the bear must have seen her unconscious body, thought she was dead, and moved on. Sometime later, I found her unconscious. Been like that most of the time she has been in my care."

"Can I assume Mrs. Adams has been properly escorted to the hospital?"

"Yes sir." I didn't mention that I practically had to order it.

"I understand you have an Indian woman with you?" He stared right at me.

"About a week ago, I found her and an old Indian being harassed by some men in Confederate rags. I … interrupted their improper party. Afraid the last one gave me a lead ball for my efforts. I'd be dead if it wasn't for the old Indian and the girl."

"Yes … We still have some trouble in the area with ex-Confederate soldiers who refuse to believe the war is over. We round them up where and when we can, but there is a lot of territory for those 'Confederate rags' to hide in." He emphasized his point by waving to a large map behind him. "What of this old Indian?"

"His granddaughter informed me that he was dying after the confrontation with the Confederate rags. Before their interruption, the old Indian was heading back to Navajo Territory to be buried with his people. While setting to the task of healing me, old age took him. The Indian girl has been with me ever since."

I deliberately changed the subject. "I have some horses to sell, compliments of the ex-Confederates. While their uniforms were rags, they kept their weapons and horses in fine shape. Would you be interested in buying some fine horses of the south?"

"The army could always use more good horses. How many do you have to sell?"

"Four, sir."

He wrote something on paper and handed it to me, "If that price seems fair to you, just hand this to my man in the outer office. He'll see you get paid for the horses. He will then see to their care."

"Sight unseen, Sir?"

"You're Calvary, son. I trust you know good horse flesh when you see it," he answered smiling.

I thanked him and left. On handing the note to the officer who had shown me into his commander's office, he opened a safe, got out some bills and handed them to me. We walked out together. In the distance, we could see the wagon sitting in front of the post hospital and the horses still tied to the back of the wagon.

Seeing a soldier approaching, the officer spoke. "Soldier, remove those horses from that wagon over there and take them to the stable master. They're now property of the U.S. Army."

"Yes, sir. Sir!" He then rushed over to the horses, untied them from the back of the wagon, and walked off with them.

"I got some extra saddles that came with those horses," I added.

"We have a rather well known trading post around the corner. They'd most likely give you good trade for them saddles."

"I thank you, sir." That business done, I moseyed over to the hospital to check on Mrs. Adams and Dawn.

After I checked to make sure Dawn was being treated well, she informed me that Mrs. Adams would eventually be fine after an unknown time in the hospital. Dawn mentioned that the doctor was interested that Mrs. Adams was a trained and experienced nurse.

"Miz. Adams have job when she heal," Dawn reported.

We made fast business of trading the used saddles for supplies, the supplies being mostly foodstuff and special ammo needed for my Henry rifle. The storekeeper apparently had had some experience trading with the local Indians, before things went bad among the Indian tribes, so he had no problems with Dawn's presence. While conducting business, I glanced through a doorway and took notice of a saloon and eating area. With business done and supplies packed into the wagon, I started inside for a big lunch. I came up short when I realized that Dawn held back.

"Let's get some some food in the diner."

"Indians not welcome where white man eat," Dawn said

"You are with me. You eat where I eat," I snapped, confidence in my words.

We started to enter by way of the trading post, when the grizzly old man that served us previously without a problem stopped our progress. "Sir, they won't allow your Indian in the diner. I have no problem with it, but they will. Just thought you should know."

I went back outside to Horse, where he was railed next to the wagon and wagon horse. I removed my Henry rifle from its saddle scabbard. I re-entered the trading post. Dawn had not walked out with me, but had stood where I left her. When she saw the rifle, she said nothing, but I noticed a slight smile appear on her stern face. The grizzly old man said nothing more as I walked into the diner with rifle in hand and Dawn right behind me.

When we entered, a fat man behind the bar yelled out, "Hey, we don't serve her type here."

I moved the Henry from a one-hand grip to a two-hand grip, without actually pointing it anywhere. "Henry here says you do now." Henry, Dawn, and I found a table and waited for service. Apparently we had arrived between the lunch crowd and the dinner crowd, because all the tables were empty, and there was only one soldier at the bar having a beer.

The fat man said something to the soldier at the bar, who then rushed out. Meanwhile, Henry, Dawn, and I continued to wait for service.

After a while, the door the soldier had left through opened and Colonel Christopher "Kit" Carson walked into the room. He looked around, taking in the whole room—the fat man behind the bar, and all the empty tables but one. Then he looked over at Henry, Dawn and I and joined us.

Smiling, Kit Carson called over to the fat man and ordered, "Chuck, get your oversized wife out here and take my friends' orders for lunch." He made a point of looking around the empty room. "I see no one complaining, do you? Before you answer that, remember I can make this place off limits to all military personal."

He calmly reached over and picked up my Henry rifle off the table, grinning. "I don't believe you'll need this with your meal." Thus said, he leaned the rifle against the side of the table as a very busty woman bounced to our table.

My new friend ordered, "Three of your biggest steaks, potatoes, and your fine fresh bread. I hope you don't mind my ordering?" The latter question was directed my way.

Seeing Dawn's discomfort, I responded, "Make that two steaks. She don't eat meat."

" May I recommend some vegetable stew for … the lady? I have a meatless soup I prepared just this morning," the portly woman suggested, staring uncomfortably at Kit Carson.

"Sounds just fine," I answered.

"How would you men like your steaks?"

Kit Carson answered, "Well done, for me."

I surprised myself when I answered, "Raw … I mean, medium rare." I had always had my steaks well done, but I really wanted this one hardly cooked at all.

After ordering water for Dawn and beers for us men, we sat to having a delightful nooner while the fat bartender steamed over cleaning his bar and glasses. Kit Carson and I shared war stories back and forth. The meal couldn't have been all that much fun for Dawn. She quietly enjoyed her meal, looking stern while occasionally sneaking glances at the grumbling fat man. Eventually we said our good-byes to the Colonel and continued our journey.

Late in the day, after encamping for the night, I set to taking care of the horses while Dawn set to building a fire and making dinner. Sitting around the fire and enjoying beans and pan bread from trade post supplies, I broke the silence.

"I figure we head for Navajo Territory?"

"No," she insisted. "I with you. You Skin-walker. Navajo fear Skin-walker. Not good go Navajo Territories."

"Not to argue, but if your Grandfather trusted me with the gift, wouldn't your people trust me as well?"

"My people no trust Skin-walker. Skin-walkers get gift from Evil One. Do evil for Him."

"How would your people even know I'm a Skin-walker?"

"Sign in eyes and way walk. Animal eyes light up at night. Your eyes light like animals even when in you in human form. You walk with stealth of killer. These things my people see in you. They fear."

"Need more learning." She then went into her bag of pelts and handed me yet another I had never seen before.

"How many pelts do you have in that bag?" I was amazed at her seemingly endless supply.

"I not know. Many," she answered with sincere honesty.

Chapter Six
~ The Clever Coyote ~

Taking the fur pelt from Dawn, I noted again that I didn't know what pelt I was holding.

Dawn broke the suspense with the directions. "Go, remove clothes, tie on pelt, think clever coyote."

I did as ordered and suddenly found myself on all fours feeling much like I did in wolf form, except a bit more playful. I ran off, exploring the area, wild and free, with no thought for anything until…

I came up short at the sound of a rattle.

A rattlesnake was in my path and there was no way around it, and I didn't want to go around it. Rattlesnake meat was good eating. Besides, I was a bit enthralled by the sound of the rattle.

As I moved toward the snake, his rattling intensified. I was enjoying that rattling sound. I was fascinated the closer I got, the harder the rattle shook, and, as I moved away, the rattling lessened. For a time, I just moved closer to and away from the rattler, enjoying how my movements changed the intensity. When I got too close, it struck out as fast as lightning, but I was faster as I jumped back out of striking range.

The rattlesnake recoiled and continued with the fun sounding rattle. Again, I tried moving in, and again the snake watched and waited to take another strike. When I was close enough, it struck again. It just missed me as I rebounded away from its deadly fangs. I knew those fangs were dripping death, but I didn't care. I was having fun making the snake rattle.

I tried moving in from one side or another, but the sneaky snake warily watched my every move, rattle a-rattling, head turning to match my every move. I tried moving in from the side, and the snake struck out at me at every turn. Failing to put the bite on me, it would recoil and prepare again, always with that delightful rattle going.

Again, I came straight on and the snake struck out with a hiss. This time, I bounded to the side and lunged, catching the back of the snake's head with my jaws. The snake was mine. I crushed the snake in my jaws and, unhappily, the fun rattle stopped its rattling. Oh, well, the fun rattle was no more, so I lay down to enjoy my snake meat dinner. After dinner, I bounded off, looking for my next adventure or my next meal.

I was almost past a bush, when I realized that a pair of eyes was carefully watching my every move. On closer examination, I was just able to make out that the eyes came with a long pair of ears, up and alert. A rabbit dinner. I moved slowly, casually, toward the eyes with long ears, but just as I got temptingly close, the rabbit jumped out from the bush and charged off. The chase was on. I chased that fun little rabbit and, just as I got close, the fun little rabbit would suddenly change direction and gain ground away from me, and the chase was on again. This kept on until it just wasn't fun anymore, so I stopped and watched the fun little rabbit run away.

I roamed mountain and canyon, enjoying the quiet freedom, when I spied a long, lean, black and white bird nesting under a desert bush. Nest meant eggs. Meat and eggs dinner.

As I snuck in toward the strange, long, black and white bird, it moved off the eggs and crouched down. I'm thinking, 'Well, maybe just eggs.' Then the bird jumped up and spread its short, rounded wings. While it was some distance from the eggs, I couldn't help but act on the challenge. As I approached, the bird took flight, running. I charged after it, but couldn't keep up. Just as I thought I might be catching up to the bird, it would change direction and shoot off, putting distance between us again. This just kept going on and on and on. A couple of times when I thought I had it, the bird would take flight, change direction, and hit the ground running, out-distancing me again. Finally, I just gave up. This bird was too hard to catch, and it just wasn't worth it. I would just satisfy myself with the eggs, except where were the eggs? In running around after the bird, I could not remember where the eggs were.

I gave up on my meal of meat and eggs, or even of my meal of just eggs.

I figured it was about time to head back to camp. On the way, I spied another one of those long, lean, black and white birds. This one had about half a rattlesnake hanging out of its mouth.

The bird was heading for an overhang, a long overhang that stretched between us. I jumped up onto the overhang and edged a few feet toward my next meal. Once in position, I just waited as it walked by. Suddenly, it was right there in my trap; I pounced and caught the bird by the neck. It was mine.

After breaking the bird's neck, I sat to eat my two meals in one, the bird and the unconsumed rest of the rattlesnake. What fun, two meals in one. After dinner, I headed to camp for real.

I arrived without any incident and made quick work of changing back to my human form and getting dressed. Inside the tepee, as I was preparing for sleep, I looked to Dawn. "You mind a question?"

"No." Never one to waste words.

"I kept coming across some strange birds. They are long, lean, and black and white with red, white and blue in the face. Fast suckers. Any idea what they are?"

"Roadrunners," she answered.

I didn't bother to inform her what good eating roadrunners could be.

Chapter Seven
~ The Great Golden Eagle ~

As the sun started setting, Dawn spoke. "Time do something different. Time to fly." Then she pulled out a belt of large brown and golden feathers.

"Lose clothes while upon wagon. Use belt and think great predator bird, think Golden Eagle!"

If it wasn't for everything that happened before this, I'd have said to Dawn, "You're crazy,'" and walked off, but I knew better, so I took the belt of feathers and did as instructed. Once I had my clothes off and the belt on, I noticed that my eye level was lower and my arms had flung out on their own. I took inventory of my arms and found great, powerful looking wings.

I performed an experimental flap of my wings and almost went backward off the wagon. It was enough for me to get the idea. So I hopped onto the wagon seat, the highest part of the wagon, gave my massive and powerful wings a flap and almost tumbled forward, over myself and off the wagon front. I hopped back on the wagon seat, turned to face the front of the wagon, and, once back into position, I gave a mighty flap of my wings while positioning upward and found myself soaring into the wild, dark sky, but even though it was dark, I could see even better than any human sees during the day.

I soared into the air, quickly getting the feel of wind drifts and my ability to use it to keep aloft with minimal effort. For hours, I just enjoyed the power of the wind and the night air and continued soaring into the heavens. Despite mostly gliding with the winds, I was growing hungry. I started looking for food in addition to discovering a whole new world as seen from high above everything and everyone. I suddenly thought of other avian creatures, but for now, the skies were all mine.

Focusing on looking for food, I flew off into the east and hadn't flown long before I heard the sounds of nervous horses corralled below. At first, I thought that even at my high flight, the horses had sensed me as a predator, and my flying over them made them nervous. I was about to fly off to give the horses their peace when I caught movement not far from the north side of the corral. I saw a cougar, and he was defiantly stalking and slinking toward the corral of horses. It looked to me the only thing holding that bad cat back was that he hadn't decided on which horse was dinner.

I might be a mighty Eagle right now, but deep down there still was a Calvary man in me. No Calvary man was going to let good horseflesh become dinner for a cougar.

I took aim at that wily cougar and swooped down on it. Unfortunately, I came in too fast, slammed into the big cat instead of on it, and sent it tumbling, and I almost tumbled with it. I succeeded in soaring back into the air. It occurred to me as we tumbled together in my tactical mistake, I almost became the cougar's dinner instead of the horse. For the sake of the horses, I had to try again, this time taking more care in my aim and in my attack.

The cougar did not want to play with me and started running away. If I let this bad cat get the better of me, what was going to keep it from returning after I flew away?

So, I took careful aim on my running target, swooped in long and low, and caught that bad cat by its hindquarters. I then went airborne, bad cat swinging between my claws.

As I had no plans for eating the cat, I just flew off with it until I spied a creek ahead. I dropped the bad cat right into the running water, so it could get its Saturday night bath. It screamed all the way down until a large splash cut it off. I circled, not out of concern for that cat, just out of interest in seeing the beast swimming for the bank.

Even though I had no plans to consume it, I discovered I was getting hungry, so I went to flying around looking for something to eat.

I hadn't looked long when I spied a scorpion coming out of its hole. While it looked edible, it didn't look palatable to my human part, so I continued looking.

Eventually, I spotted a long-eared rabbit that either was at rest or had discovered my flying shadow cast by the moon. I took careful aim and swooped down on it. Just as my talon struck, the rabbit darted sideways and took off!

I gained altitude while looking for that speedy little dinner—I mean rabbit. Eventually, I spotted the little meal running with all its might. I took careful aim to swoop in and down, behind the running rabbit. Just as my talons were about to crush down on my scared little dinner, it dodged sideways again, temporarily escaping my hungry claws.

This dinner was not going to be as easy to catch as I thought.

Again, I gained elevation enough to turn, and, taking aim, I swooped down on the scared little rabbit, and just as it was about to dodge again, I lunged out with my talons and caught me some dinner. I landed and went about enjoying raw rabbit. As a human, I had enjoyed well-cooked rabbit many times. It was interesting to taste how enjoyable raw rabbit tasted instead.

After enjoying my dinner, I was happy and eager to regain the bliss of the air. I decided it was about time to head back to camp, but before I could, I just had to look after those corralled horses and see if they were still safe for the night. I noticed my flight took me back over the area where I had dropped that old cougar and observed that the beastie was nowhere to be seen, even from the air.

I finally found myself over the area of the horses and discovered why they were corralled. The horses were in a permanent corral just outside of a good-sized Indian encampment. This encampment was not far from where Dawn and I had set up camp.

Remembering what she had warned about staying away from her people and Indians in general, I decided we were going to move. Northward looked clear of Indians and other human traffic. It also looked easy wagon traveling, so northward it would be. Flying back to camp, I realized that we didn't want to move so far northward that we would have to contend with a cold winter. I had spent some very harsh winters camping out in the cold during my war years and was not interested in repeating the experience.

I flew back to camp without any incidents. After changing back to human form, I jumped down to stand next to the wagon. I made quick work of getting my clothes together and quicker work of getting dressed.

In the morning, I informed Dawn of the Indian village not far to the west and of the apparent easy trail going north. We pitched camp and started traveling north into the Colorado territories, not knowing we'd be moving from the grease pan into the cook fire.

With Dawn directing the wagon and me riding ahead of the wagon atop Horse, we headed north. While keeping watch up ahead, I could not help but wonder at how much fun it would be to be leading this caravan from high in the sky, on the wings of an eagle.

Chapter Eight
~ Somewhere in the Colorado Territories ~

I guessed we were a few days into Colorado territories, keeping the breathtaking mountain ranges to our left and the open prairie land ahead. We had crossed a used trail and followed it, which had made for a very peaceful, scenic, and lonely trip until …

In the distance, we saw the outline of a tall figure on horseback. I pulled up Horse, and, as the wagon seat reached my side, Dawn halted the wagon. There we sat waiting to see what or who this distant stranger was. I loosened my Union holster in case I needed to get to my Colt quickly.

"Not Indian," Dawn said.

I kind of figured that, with the big floppy hat that the distant silhouette wore. While I wasn't real knowledgeable about Indians, it seemed to me Indians preferred traveling on ponies, not the large standing steed silhouetted before us.

"Greetings. Mind if I come forward. I'm of no harm to you and your lady," the stranger called out.

"Come ahead, just don't make any fast movement with that big .50 you're toting across your saddle."

He came forward slowly, careful not to raise alarm. "I see you know your firearms. It's also wise to travel prepared. Jim Baker's the name."

This Jim Baker sat tall in the saddle, all dressed in buckskins and a large-brim felt hat, with a long percussion rifle resting across his saddle horn. I noted his hand was well away from the trigger.

"Hello, Jim Baker. I'm Cody O'Conner, and this woman beside me is Dawn."

"Wife? I've had a number of squaw wives in my time. One was a

36

Cheyenne woman, which is why I can travel these parts in ... some safety."

"Just a friend and traveling companion," I answered.

"Navajo. She's not going to make your traveling north any easier. The Sioux and the Cheyenne have had their fill of white man, white man lies, and white man breaking treaties. When 'blue bellies' start making forts within their sacred hunting grounds, the arrows are going to fly and fly heavy."

"Any suggestions on evading contact with the Indian trouble?" This mountain man, Jim Baker seemed a person who would be aware of this area.

"It's still plenty early enough to travel through the mountains before winter sets in."

"I had thought of going far enough north to visit Denver City. Got a hankering for a little vacation from the country life I have been living lately."

"Well, the city is the place right now: The whole township of Denver City is celebrating its establishment as permanent seat of government by territorial legislature. Talk is if Colorado ever becomes a state, Denver City could be its capital city.

"As for the Indians, if you stay north on this trail, with the mountains close at your side, you have a good chance of getting to Denver City without trouble. If you drift eastward, you could stumble into Indian trouble. I heard there's current trouble to the east and northeast of Denver City. There is no Indian trouble in Denver City.

"Just keep the mountains close on your west side until the whole damn plain opens in front of you then go west until a river gets in your way. Just follow that river south into the mountains, and you will run right into Denver City. Boy, you just be a remembering to stay out of the plains proper. The Indians got it in their heads it's theirs, and they will skin you if they find you in their territory."

"Thanks for the information and the advice."

"One more piece of advice, for what it's worth. Don't go into Denver City with your traveling companion. Indians aren't welcome there."

I looked to Dawn, who just nodded once, saying nothing aloud, but saying plenty otherwise. When I broke the news to Dawn of my plans to visit Denver City, she just nodded.

"I camp away from white man city. Wait return."

We said our good-byes to Jim Baker, mountain man, and, taking his advice, stayed on the trail, which hung close to the mountains. As the mountain man said, we had no trouble with the Indians all the way to Denver City.

When we guessed we were somewhere northeast and within miles of Denver City, we stopped and set up camp a distance off trail. With the horses seen to, the tepee up, and most of the items Dawn would be a needing for a spell unpacked from the wagon, I changed into an Eagle and scouted the area by air.

I had two goals in mind, scout the area for any Indians that might be close by and check the trail to Denver City by air. I flew around the encampment for miles, carefully looking for any signs of Indian raiding parties and found no signs of any Indians at all. I continued circling for a while, but the only signs of life I spotted were critters that looked quite tasty, but I decided dinner could wait because I wanted a bird's eye view of Denver City before it got dark.

Following the river from the air, I finally come in sight of Denver City, and what a sight it was! The city was already spread out for miles in every direction. Some of the streets had permanent blocks of tall brick buildings. Other parts had blocks of tent towns within the city limits. From the air, the streets looked unpaved, but well cared for. I counted four buildings that looked like churches; I even took a break on the top of one church building's cross while eagle-eyeing the city.

Flying closer to the tent town, I found what interested me, an area of saloons, gambling houses, and the tenderloin (area designated for the fallen doves). I couldn't help shiver at the thought of my ma even knowing I knew anything of the tenderloin or fallen doves. Still, it had been some time since I felt a soft bed and a warm woman, and it was definitely on my schedule.

After a once-around the city, I flew off to get me a meaty dinner or two and get back to where I left Dawn encamped before night fell. Then I wanted a good night's sleep before heading into the big city come the rising of the morning sun.

Before arriving at camp, I ate a nice fox. He was a little challenging to catch, but I was getting the hang of swooping in for the kill. He was easier to catch than the last rabbit I hooked in my talons. While enjoying my meal, my mind wondered on a large steak, potatoes, and fresh bread, all washed down with a nice cold beer.

Don't get me wrong. I was enjoying my fresh raw meat meals in my various beastly forms; I was just looking forward to a more human-style meal that I wasn't going to get from my non-meat-eating traveling companion, now that I was good and healthy. These days, if I wanted a meaty meal, I had to catch it myself or go into town to get one. I sure couldn't complain about Dawn's great breakfast breads she was prone to make. Some of her great breakfast bread and a cup of thick black coffee could really get you going.

On my flight back to camp, I came across a nice long snake for dessert and still made it back before dark. Before ending my current adventures as the great Golden Eagle, I made some recon flights over the area of our encampment, looking for any signs of Indians and again found none. As I was about to end my recon of the area, I spied a distant strand of a dust cloud, the type an Indian raiding party could make, so I flew off to put an eagle eye on the potentially dangerous situation.

As I neared, I was pleasantly surprised to spy a wild herd of bison apparently on the move from one grazing ground to another. Though I was full from my hunting meals, the predator bird in me couldn't help but consider how tasty one of those big bison would be, even though such a beast would be much too big a meal to take down as an eagle and certainly too much meat for one meal. I enjoyed the sight of the herd on the move for a bit and then flew back to the encampment, to rest and recuperate for my big city trip.

Back in human form, I assured Dawn there was no sign of any Indian activity in the immediate area outside of herself. I was a bit glad that Dawn was the quiet Indian type, not prone to filling me in on her days. I was one tired human after all that flying around I had been doing. Not surprising, considering all the ground I had covered that day. Despite the lack of alarming evidence of trouble in the area, I still slept with my side arm easily at hand.

Chapter Nine
~ Denver City ~

As the sun was rising over the plains, I was too excited about going to Denver City to properly acknowledge such a beautiful morning, let alone enjoy its splendor.

I eagerly jumped onto Horse's saddle.

"Captain Cody ..."

My exuberant dash toward the big city grounded to a halt by a voice as attention commanding as any superior officer I ever faced during the war. I have long since given up on just getting her to call me "Cody."

"Captain Cody, when return?"

"It kinda depends on how Lady Luck smiles down on me at the poker tables," I answered, smiling. The thought did cross my mind for a moment. I'm glad my mother wasn't around to find out her "good boy" learned how to play poker in the army, not to mention the womanizing.

The frown on Dawn's face also reminded me of my ma. "A couple of days to a week at the most. I assume you'll be all right here for that long."

That old stern look returned to her face. "Fine. Go."

So I did as ordered, and, digging my heels into Horse's side, I was off to the adventures in the big city. Remembering the way well from my aerial reconnaissance as an eagle, I had no problems or misadventures getting to Denver City. I came into the city by way of the tent town, which I knew led to the more despicable part of town and all the things I was most looking forward to doing on my leave.

The first thing I did was ride up to a stable house to see to Horse's keeping, since I would be roaming the city on foot. As I rode up, an old codger came out to meet me and, from his worn-out duds, I could see I had come to the right place. Among other things, he wore grey pants with a stripe down the outer legs. The pants said ex-Confederate, but the stripe down the pants said a fellow Cavalryman, a man who knew horses.

"Hey, nice horse you got there, mister," he said as I was dismounting.

"Thanks, Horse, Horse is his name, we've seen many a battle together, and we're still mates. I know many a man who can't say that."

"Yep, I kind of figured that from the way you and he rode up here, like you know what you're doing. You'd be surprised how many wanna-be miners come riding in here looking like they're not even sure which end of their ride is the thinking part. If two bits a day keep is fine with you, just waltz him on in here, and we'll get him fixed up comfy-like in a nice clean stall. I require at least two bits now, just in case you come back with nothing but your clothes after the gambling houses get to you."

"That's fine," I said, pulling out the money.

"Just leave your saddle and blanket on the stall wall. I'd suggest you empty them there saddle holsters of their contents and take them with you, not that you'll be needing them, I'm just not going to be responsible for such."

"Can you recommend a good hotel to hold up in during my stay?"

"The Grand is as good as any and better than most. It even has its own bathhouse just out the back door for a fee. Get a room and the fee's half off. It's just down a block and across the street. If you've a mind for some new duds, there's The Trader that's right on the way. They fix you right nicely, Cap."

"How do you know my rank?"

"Kind of figured you carry yourself like a Captain. That's to say an officer that knows his stuff, not a high-ranking, book-stuffed phony!"

"Second Regimental Cavalry, Kansas City," I answered, putting my hand out.

"Company K, Second Texas Cavalry … Confederate Army. I won't hold that blue hat of yours against you, if you don't hold my gray britches against me, deal?"

"Deal." I smiled in return. With the full knowledge that Horse was going to be well cared for, I left him behind to start my vacation proper.

While heading for the hotel with the intent of getting a room with a warm bed and a warmer bathtub, I got derailed at the site of "The

Trader," thinking that it really would be nice to have some nice clean clothes to change into after a much-needed bath. You can't get clothes much cleaner then new. So I headed into "The Trader" where a little man in glasses, dressed to manage a shop, was very glad to refit me completely from unmentionables, to a shirt and jeans, to a silk bandana that matched the jeans in color. A little la-de-da, but the price was right. Buy the jeans and the matching bandana went with it.

I walked into "The Trader" with my saddlebags hanging over my shoulder and my Sharps and Henry Repeater in hand. I left "The Trader" with my saddlebags hanging over my shoulder, my Sharps and Henry Repeater in one hand, and a bundle of new clothes all wrapped and properly tied up with string in the other. Now, on to the Grand Hotel.

Maybe because it was early morning, but I couldn't help but be surprised at how quiet the streets were. The whole city had been much busier when I had checked it out from above. When I thought about it, my aerial recon had been during later hours, and the whole city then was bustling with activity. While I mused over what difference the time of day must make in the city, I found myself approaching the Grand Hotel. So, after taking one more look around the block, I entered.

After I stepped into the entrance lobby, I took a moment to glance over the place. Straight ahead, a middle-aged brunette woman manned the hotel desk. She had her back to me with an open ledger on the front desk and a bank of key/mail holders in front of her. To her right was a stairway that most likely led up to the hotel rooms. To her left was an open doorway that led into a dining area. I could smell steaks, fresh bread, and beer wafting from that direction. It made me hungry.

I would have to check out the mess hall later. Immediately to her left was a doorway that opened onto darkness. I remembered about the bathhouse being in the back of the place and figured the doorway led out back to it. I'd definitely have to ask about the bathhouse.

I walked up and dropped my weapons on the desk. The industrious lady gave me a quick once over.

"Looking for a room?"

"A room and a bath," I answered.

"The rooms are fifty cents a night, with a deposit of one dollar up front. For an additional dollar, you can walk right through that doorway and my husband will fix you right up with a hot tub of water, soap, and some sweet smelling stuff to finish you off. The bath is half what it would cost if you don't have a room."

I pulled out three dollars and ordered a room and a bath.

"For no extra charge I could lock-up your shootin'-irons. You won't need them here. We have Sheriff Pollock. He's real good and mean about keeping the peace around here. Any trouble and he'll lock you up."

"I don't recall seeing a jailhouse in Denver City while having a look around."

She gave me a delightful little laugh. "We don't have a jailhouse proper. Get in trouble and he'll lock you up in his hotel and charge you a dollar a night for your interment."

I saw no reason to carry my long-arms around with me, but I'd feel plum naked without my sidearm. Not bothering to mention my extra Colt in my saddlebag, I slid the two long-arms her way. "Sounds fine: lock up my rifles, but I'll keep my sidearm. Don't plan on needing it, I'd just feel nak … pardon, I mean, I'd feel undressed without it."

"Fine, just be sure not to use it here. Sheriff Pollock might just throw you in his hotel and forget all about you." She plucked a key from the board behind her. "Here, your room is 202. Rooms are up those steps. When you're ready for that bath just head around through that doorway and my husband will fix you right up."

I figured I'd get right to that bath, so I did as instructed and found myself walking through a short walled tunnel, then through a door I had to open. Then I found myself in a large room with four large tubs of water, none in use. Further back was a large stove with a fire going over a large metal pan. In a corner, a fat little gent read a paper, which he tossed to the ground.

"Put your things and your clothes on a bench of your choice and get yourself into a tub, and I'll heat the water for you …"

After a nice long hot bath, I cut open the bundle of new clothes and got dressed. Now, I looked good for my vacation. My old clothes got rolled and stuffed in my saddlebag. Next on the schedule, a nice large steak and eggs, and a cold beer in the dining area. Traveling with Dawn, I might get eggs for breakfast on occasion, but never a breakfast of steak and eggs from that squaw.

Though I hadn't yet seen my room, so far the old-timer at the stables had not sold me a bad bill of goods. I'd gotten some good deals on my new duds at The Trader, and here at The Grand Hotel, I'd gotten a great bath and an even better feed-on in their dining room.

I was relaxing with a full stomach and a second beer while debating whether I should hit a gambling house first and then the local "cat-house," or hit the "cat-house" first, just to make sure I had the money for that warm bed and a warmer woman. I was just too full of lunch to make such important decisions, so I left the diner for my hotel room to wait for the evening when the town, at least this part of town, will wake up.

The room wasn't bad. It had a large comfortable-looking bed, nice-looking furniture in the form of a dresser with a mirror, and a table and chairs. Wallpaper covered the walls and drapes framed the windows. The room was cozy even though nothing matched. Cozy enough that I took a comfy nap to work off my nooner.

Hours later, I woke feeling fresh and ready to face the night's adventure. From what I could see and hear out the open window of my room, the city nightlife hadn't waited for me. It already sounded a lot busier in the streets than it did earlier.

I put on my boots, strapped on my sidearm, threw my hat on my head, and left my room and the hotel feeling a bit like a boy on Christmas morning. Adding to the feeling of festiveness was the hustle and bustle of a busy street that earlier in the day had been so dead. Carts and wagons toted fine dressed men and women. Men on horseback meandered past men and woman coming and going on fancy buckboards, and people galore walked and rushed around everywhere. There wasn't a building on the street that wasn't lit up to the nines, enticing folks to come on in and have a grand-old-time.

Down the street was a finely lit place with the glaring sign that beckoned one and all to "The Lucky Strike." That looked like the place for me. So The Lucky Strike it was.

I walked up to the saloon batwing doors, but had to stop and take in all the hustle and bustle of the well-lit place. To the left was a long bar that took up the whole side of the large rectangular room, with two to three very busy bartenders. I had never seen such a large bar in all my days. Behind the bartenders were wall-to-wall liquor bottles of many shapes, sizes, and colors. The display of booze was split in two with a large mirror in the middle, a mirror large enough for many a man to watch himself get drunk.

Games of chance took up the rest of the room. In the back, I could see roulette wheels. I could both see and hear the craps table and could almost hear them bones a-rolling. I could see blackjack tables and other tables where I was sure poker betting was commencing. Betting sounded like a grand idea, so I entered and started performing a recon of the tables.

The place was so full that some men were neither at a gambling table nor at the bar. In passing, I overheard something strange enough to catch my ear. Someone called O'Brannen was so desperate he went into those mountains looking for gold.

"Didn't you try to stop him?" one man said.

"Sure, I reminded him of all those who had gone before and had never returned," another replied.

"What did he say?"

"He said it was just stories to keep miners away from the real gold. He said he'd be willing to bet he'd come back with so much gold, he'd disappear to go off and live the high life."

"He was a good …"

I stopped my eavesdropping and continued my recon of the place. I was here to do some gambling. I'd made my rounds at least once when I came to a poker table that had a dude who looked like he was gambling away his gold strike for the week and was about to have to return to his mining.

Sure enough, he only lasted a couple of additional hands when he tapped out and grudgingly gave up his seat. Sincerely hoping the dude was just a bad player and not occupying an unlucky seat, I sat down and joined the game. My table companions looked like a couple of cattle hands and a business-type dude by their clothes. I had observed no one at the table was playing like a professional gambler.

As I made my observations, the cards started flowing. I wasn't playing long when an attractive, skimpily dressed young woman asked if anyone would like something from the bar. I ordered a beer and the two cattle hands said that sounded like a good idea and ordered the same. Then, the game began.

Hours later, after winning more hands than losing, I had a pile of money in front of me and had helped drain a businessman of his pot. An old-timer who I guessed was either a mountain man or a gold miner replaced him. Then, the game began again.

During my early war years, I'd had a sergeant that trained me well in the game of poker, at some considerable cost to my military pay, I might add. If you think of poker as a game of chance, you shouldn't be playing. I wasn't winning every hand, but I was doing very nicely from the looks of the growing pile of money in front of me.

I was starting to think about taking a break when a very attractively dressed young woman brushed her large, half-naked breasts against me. "You look like a man who would enjoy a sport of a different, private kind."

Looking sideways from my cards to that luscious pair of soft melons, I could hardly argue with the woman whose dress I was practically looking down. Looking up into those deep blue eyes did the deal.

I threw down my cards, which was a losing hand anyway, and picked up my money. "Sorry gents, time for a more manly game."

She walked through the crowded gambling tables with ease and grace, showing a lot of practice. Following right behind her, I didn't miss a single sway of her gorgeous hips. Finally, we cleared the full corral of gambling tables to be met with a stairway to the upper level. Heading up the stairway, I removed my gaze from my current prey's form to look up toward a well-lit hallway of gaslights and portraits, most likely not found in any decent home, and many closed doors.

As we traveled down the hallway, I found it interesting to note none of the doors had room numbers, but my tour director into my next adventure knew from practice which door to open.

The room was totally in the dark except for a little light coming in from an open window. I happened to take notice of a nice-looking balcony just outside the window. I was turning my attention to my tour director, who was making for the dresser and a gas lamp that I assumed she was going to turn on, when she quickly pulled open the top drawer and removed a pistol.

She pointed the pistol right at my face. "So you have finally come for me," she yelled, fear now painting her face, "Just like my parents claimed you would if I pursued this way of life. So, Demon, you have finally come to take me to HELL!"

I threw up my hands in surrender. "Ma'am, what are you going on about? I'm no demon, and I have no idea what you're talking about."

She waved the gun at my face. "I'm about to send you to hell alone," she shouted. "I'm about to disappoint your boss, the Devil, when you find yourself back in hell without dragging little Patty at your side.

"I saw those glowing eyes ... those demonic eyes of yours. My parents warned me how you can tell a demon in man form, by those demonic hellfire eyes of yours."

Dawn had warned me that her people, the Navajo, might discern me as a Skin-walker by my eyes. She said my eyes not only have the predatory power to see in the dark like an animal, but also will shine backlight like a wild animal. She hadn't warned me about this.

Looking down at the gun wavering in the woman's hand, I felt a little reassured that she wasn't an experienced shooter—not the way she was waving the pistol around. Then I caught the action of her finger slowly tightening on the trigger. I turned from her and dove out the open window for the balcony as a shot rang out, just squeezing past me without doing any harm to me, at least this time.

Hitting the balcony, I rolled sideways away from the window as a second shot went, I don't know where it landed, but not in me. Before she could get off another shot rang out. I lunged for the balcony railing, grabbed hold, and jumped over the railing with the intent on coming down feet first on the horse railing and bouncing off it to hit the ground running.

It almost worked. I lost it a little coming off the horse railing and hit the ground rolling to my feet. Hearing her screams coming from above, I charged away from the screams that would eventually be heard and would draw attention, even over the din from the gambling below. Dodging for the shadows of the buildings, I quickly put the whole thing behind me.

After making my escape without any sign of pursuit, I changed my pace to a walk, hanging in the shadows like a ghoul, very confused and concerned about being seen around people at night, like now.

Shaken from the experience, I got to wondering. Was I destined to have to hide from people at night? Would I have to spend the rest of my life worried I'd look strange to people during the evening hours? How many more folks would I scare just by looking at them in subdued light? Was I to go through the rest of my life looking like some freakish wild thing during the evening hours?

I decided I would just head back to my room and call it a night. In the morning, I'd pack up, get breakfast, and fetch Horse, all in the safety of daylight.

The sun was halfway to its highest point as Horse and I left the quiet Denver City behind us. Next destination, Dawn's encampment. While we traveled, it weighed heavily on me whether I would tell Dawn what happened or not, and whether I would seek her advice on the situation or not. I just couldn't decide. After all, how many people are out there looking for a person with demonic eyes?

The trail back seemed longer than the trail to Denver City. Same trail, different attitude, I guessed.

The sun was high in the sky when I got to thinking I should be seeing Dawn's tepee in the distance. After a while, I kicked Horse into picking up the pace, starting to get real concerned that something wasn't right. If I didn't come across Dawn's encampment soon, I might find a place to tie down Horse, shed some clothes, and do an eagle recon. Except of course, I didn't have my feather belt to make such a change.

Then in the distance, I was sure I saw Dawn's wagon in the horizon... I should have seen the top of her tepee long before I saw her wagon. I gave Horse a kick and a "Charge!" and we raced on toward Dawn's distant wagon.

As we neared, I could definitely see Dawn's wagon, and it was in one piece, but not the tepee. We continued racing up to the encampment...

It was a disaster.

As we rode up, I pulled on Horse's reins, but was out of the saddle and on my feet running to the destroyed tepee before Horse had come to a proper stop.

"Dawn? Dawn. Are you here anywhere? DAWN!" I was fighting to keep from losing it. I was yelling loud enough to wake the dead, but no answer was coming.

I was beginning to feel a little relieved at not seeing anything that remotely looked like an elongated lump of a body lying around. So I attacked the shreds that were once a tepee, hoping to find Dawn among the ruins while at the same time hoping not to find her. After a comprehensive, yet frantic, search of the tepee ruins, I found nothing but the ruins of our supplies. One thing that occurred to me was that I hadn't found the pelt bag that contained all my magical pelts needed to change into my various beastly forms.

I was trying to look in all directions at once. It looked like a tornado had torn through, but the wagon told the lie to that. Supplies were thrown everywhere. A closer examination proved that everything had been gone over with the sharp blades of crazed knives. I also discovered hoofed tracks, many hoofed tracks, many unshod hoofed tracks. Indians.

While I was out vacationing and having a great time, Dawn had been attacked by a band of Indians.

I made a strong effort to keep my mind on carefully searching through the ruins for any clues as to what had happened to Dawn. Her absence was a strong indication she had been taken. The question was, where did they take her? It wasn't easy. Images of horror stories I had heard over the years of the tortures Indians forced on their captives kept trying to muddle my thoughts. I made a strong effort to keep them locked away. I needed all my attention for finding Dawn.

Chapter Ten
~ A Skin-walker's Revenge ~

A more careful recon of the area told me two things—three unshod horses rode into the encampment, meaning an Indian party of three. Four unshod horses rode out, meaning the Indian party of three took Dawn alive on her horse. Careful examination showed that the four horses that rode out all contained about the same weight on them, so all four horses had riders, Dawn being one of them.

I got to thinking how easy it would be to track those horses down as a wolf. I got to wishing hard they hadn't taken the pelt bag. I got to wishing I could change into a wolf, track those Indians, and retrieve Dawn. I... suddenly found myself on all fours, my hands tripping over my clothes. I stretched out my arm in such a way that my paw came clear of my clothes, my wolf paw.

I had wished myself into a change, and I didn't have the magical pelts that were needed or so I had been told. Currently in wolf form and hampered by human clothes, I was going nowhere fast. So, I wished myself back into human form, and, completing the change with thought alone, I was human again. I quickly ran Horse toward the temporary corral that remained intact, got him unharnessed, and gave him water and feed, leaving extra of both, enough to last a couple of days.

With Horse settled, I rushed over to the wagon and ripped off my clothes. I hid them away in the wagon under a canvas and wished myself again into wolf form.

On all fours, I took to tracking the trail of the four horses, the Indians and Dawn. I was quickly traveling over miles of some of the most breathtaking land God ever laid out, but all I could lose my breath over was the trail of four horses that appeared to be moving at a fairly good pace by the distance between hoof tracks. I followed the trail for most of the day, only taking one break for some water at the riverside, because I didn't know when another chance would come. The four horsemen might have canteens with them, but I didn't.

I kept tracking the trail of hooves for most of the day. Late into the afternoon, I came upon a promising sight: a pile of horse droppings. I could smell it was still fairly fresh, but I pawed it lightly and discovered that it was also fairly soft, meaning it hadn't even been laying around long enough for the sun to bake it hard. I knew I must be gaining on my quarry. I was not far from them.

As the sun started to set, I spied a mountainous area ahead, and the tracks appeared to be heading straight for it. I continued to follow the horse trail, as it got closer to the mountain area. As the sun set and it was getting darker, I started to fear losing the trail after coming so far. I felt a stab of fear I might lose Dawn. I shook it off like a wet dog shakes off water and continued forward.

As I neared the mountainous area, I saw an opening within the hilly mounds possibly a canyon within. I continued ahead.

Still traveling the horse trail and getting close to an opening into the mountainous area, I smelled smoke and water. I'd have bet anything my quarry was there.

Coming closer to the opening, I started stalking the entrance when I noticed a ridge about eight to ten feet up that contained an area wide enough to traverse. It possibly was a way in that would allow me to stalk and spy on the area within from overhead.

I figured if I thought myself into wolf form and back to human without the pelt maybe I could change to other forms. I wished myself to be an eagle, and, with one mighty flap of my wings, swooped up onto the overhang. Once there, I wished myself to become coyote form because the coyote form was sleeker, smaller, and stealthier. I quickly found my large powerful wings changed to two mighty coyote paws.

I stalked in slowly and quietly. I started to hear talk. It was Indian talk, so I had no way of understanding what was being said. As I neared, I came within sight of a campfire, with four forms sitting around it. Two logs had been moved up near the campfire, one log on either side of it, with two people per log. As I stalked closer, I made out a form more clothed than the other half-naked forms around the fire. The fully dressed form seemed to have its hands in the lap together in an unnatural way. Of course, it had to be Dawn with her hands bound together in front of her.

She seemed to be in no danger, so I just watched for some time, trying to figure some way to separate her from her three captors. I was starting to get frustrated with my lack of ideas that could safely separate her without any harm coming to her, when something interesting happened.

One of the captors got up and moved away from the others. His walk took him well away from them, and out of sight of the group camped around the fire. I watched as he walked up close to the mountain wall, and eventually I was only able see him because of my superior night sight, as he was walking well away from the fire, well away from the others. I watched him lower his rawhide britches and lean down. While he was busy with his call of nature, I slowly and carefully crept up the overhang until I was practically over his head.

With a thought, I changed into my mightier wolf form. Either he heard something or smelled something of my approach, because he came to his feet slowly, obviously carefully listening for life signs and sounds in the dark. As he started to turn, I noticed he was cautiously unsheathing his knife from his side.

With a low growl escaping my throat, I lunged at the lonely Indian even as he was turning my way, raising his knife with the purpose of plunging it into the fiend in the dark, preparing to plunge his sharp tool of death into me.

He didn't get a chance.

I hit him in the chest, with the full force of my large wolf form plummeting down on him. Before he could plunge his knife into my side, I strategically turned my head just right so that I had his throat in my powerful jaws before we hit the ground. I snapped my jaws down on his throat in such a way that I heard his throat snap like a branch under a ton of boulders.

As we hit the ground, I rolled away from the dead form of my first human victim as the Skin-walker, his throat gushing crimson fluid into the dry ground.

I held my ground, listening carefully to see if the attack had been heard from the campfire. No sounds of alarm came.

It was now down to two of them against one of me, and I still had the problem of removing those two heathens from Dawn without her being harmed. Time had now become an issue. I would have to come up with a plan before the two missed their dead friend. I crept close enough to see the encampment and got an idea, a big idea.

Changing into my smaller coyote form, I snuck around to creep carefully up to the campfire from behind the two Indians sitting close together.

When I was in position behind the two redskins, I rose up like a great demon from hell and let loose a grizzly bear roar that slammed off the mountain walls with such force that it returned, slamming into the two redskins that were springing to their feet and spinning my way. Seeing a giant, angry grizzly bear right behind them, one had the sense to grab his lance while coming to his feet. He made a move with the lance that I blocked with such force as to send lance and lancer flying to the ground.

The other redskin in front of me just froze at my nearness. I had plans for him. I placed my giant front paws on each side of his head and squeezed, oh so slowly. Blood started pouring out of his nose, then his mouth, and as the flow got stronger, his eyes popped out, and blood started pouring from his eyeholes. I then dug both of my claws into his neck and, with one strong pull, separated his head from the rest of him. As his body dropped to the ground, blood now spouting from his neck hole, I tossed his head into the fire. The greasy, hairy head ignited in flame and then rolled from the fire over to Dawn's feet.

Wide-eyed but still sitting on her log, Dawn moved enough to keep from being burned by the flaming skull, while eyeing me in a way I couldn't read. She had made no sound, possibly because of the gag stuffed in her mouth and tied in place. I moved toward her and, in one slice of my powerful single claw, freed her bound hands. Her look past me reminded me there was still one more Indian to kill, an Indian that was charging me with his lance fully extended in front of him.

I slashed a paw sideways with such energy that the lance broke, sending the majority of the spear-tipped weapon flying off into the dark. With the other paw, I slashed upward, right through his chest like hot knives through butter. My powerful claws of death continued, slamming upward out of his chest to catch his jaw, which I then pulled with such force toward myself, that I ripped his jaw right out from his face. I tossed it away.

The lancer just stood there, bug-eyed, with one row of teeth gleaming in the firelight. Suddenly, his eyes rolled up and his body dropped.

As my first victim was closest to some flowing water, I moved off into his direction, going up to the running water to change back into human form. I had lots of blood splattered all over me to wash off. After cleaning myself from the very cold mountain stream of water, I went over to my first victim and, for modesty's sake, relieved the corpse of his buckskin britches, moccasins, and rawhide belt with knife sheath. The latter was needed to keep up the britches. Since I was wearing the knife sheath, I took a couple of minutes to find the knife. Upon my success in finding the redskin's knife, I put the knife back where it belonged.

I then strolled back to the fireside encampment. I was a little scared about what reaction would come from Dawn, who had just watched me, in grizzly bear form, rip two humans literally to pieces.

On reaching the fire, Dawn just looked at me with that expression I could not read. I set about removing the dead from the immediate area to avoid being bothered by their decaying, ghastly forms. I moved all three into a far corner of the canyon, the spot furthest possible from the fire and furthest possible from us. I did not intend to bury them. After we left the area, they would probably get to stinking bad enough to attract some critters that would take care of them the natural way.

Afterward, I cleaned up the site of all possible gore and then just sat down on the log the two Indians had vacated upon my rude entrance, waiting for Dawn to make the first move. I studied the fire patiently, waiting for a rebuke for my violence, or a rebuke about letting the dark side of Skin-walker out. I knew Indian ways enough not to expect flattery for coming to her aid, or even a thank you for rescuing me.

I couldn't have been more surprised when she broke the silence with, noticeable awe in her voice. "What did ... not possible.

"Many tales of Skin-walkers change at a thought, no pelts, no belts. Take many years' experience. You change in seconds. I saw you change from clever coyote to fearsome grizzly bear too fast for eyes. Capt. Cody, I see change."

Looking into the fire, she spoke in her more usual flat tone. "You not long Denver City."

"You could say that," I said. "Sometime, I should share my experience with you, but not tonight. I had been watching for a while. You seem unharmed, and your captors appeared intent on keeping their distance from you. Like you scared them or something."

"They found bag of pelts. They feared it, feared me Skin-walker. They not know what do with me. They talk. Take me to Chiefs. Let Chiefs deal with feared Skin-walker."

"Were your captors expecting any company, anyone else that was possible traveling with them? Any chance they were waiting for additional members of their hunting party?"

"No."

"Then I suggest we get some sleep, and head back to what's left of our encampment in the morning."

With a single nod, she agreed, and we both settled to sleeping on the ground, near the fire. One of my victims had left a wolf-skin containing his bow and arrows. Not experienced with such weapons, I slept while keeping the knife close at hand just in case. I must admit I was feeling more naked from the absence of my side arm then I was from wearing the skins I had acquired from the redskin earlier.

In the morning, we breakfasted on food my victims from the night before had left behind. Afterward, I fetched two horses, one that I recognized as Dawn's. The two we didn't have use for, I set free. It would not have gone well for us to be caught on the open plains with a bunch of Indian ponies in tow. The horses only came with horse blankets, which concerned me a little because I hadn't ridden a horse without a proper saddle since I was a kid.

I noticed that Dawn had two wolfskin quivers full of bows and arrows and apparently planned on keeping both. She was also carrying the skin bag of pelts that I had previously used to change into my beastly forms, but apparently no longer needed. I could only guess she knew how to use the bow and arrows.

We made good time in getting back to our encampment by back trailing the hoof tracks that had led her captors and me to Dawn just the day before. This time, I was able to take some time to enjoy the scenery, even though I had to keep one eye on the trail to get back to our encampment and not get lost on these wide and wonderful plains. I was also keeping a wary eye out for distant company that could be other Indian parties out and about. I was feeling all too uncomfortable dressed in stolen Indian clothes, lightly armed, and on an Indian pony.

On arriving at the encampment, I saw to the horses, which also allowed me to look in on Horse, who was as glad to see me as I was to see him. He was still well supplied with food and water. While I saw to the horses, Dawn set to work straightening our encampment and inventorying our destroyed supplies. We would be sleeping out in the open tonight and for a while because the tepee would take time to repair.

Horses cared for, I moseyed over to the wagon where I dug out my clothes, including boots, hat, and holster, and went back to the area near the horses that provided privacy to change. I didn't know why, but after changing, I rolled up the Indian clothes and placed them in a war bag I had taken from the redskin encampment. I could only guess it was a deep-seated teaching often heard from my ma, "Waste not, want not."

We both called it a night early, with nothing being said about continuing my Skin-walker education. All day and into the night, Dawn had said nothing about how I had dispatched her captors right in front of her. You'd have thought seeing a man's head ripped from his body and watching another man ripped to pieces was a daily event for an Indian woman.

By the time I awoke the next day, it was time for our nooner over beans and water. Dawn filled me in on our status. "Last a few days, longer if your wild side feed you. Maybe go Denver City, resupply."

"Can't," I exclaimed, yet I could not very well tell her why I couldn't go back to Denver City. I couldn't very well tell her the law might want me for terrorizing women as a monster. What did come to me was the mountain man.

"Remember, the mountain man told us you would not be welcomed in Denver City. After what happened the last time I went to Denver City, I sure can't leave you here again while I go to town to resupply."

"You no go back." She finished my excuses, as if she'd been there to see what happened. "Indians go north, but first travel east. Avoid bluecoat fort. We travel northeast, we find fort. If no supplies there, they tell us where we supply."

That must have been the longest I had ever heard her speak.

"We have money for supplies?" she enquired.

"We have funds and then some," I boasted, thinking back on how well my gambling had gone. Then it occurred to me the little busty number was probably sent my way to get me away from my winning ways.

It was decided that we would pack up our encampment early the next day and move on. Waiting till the next day would, among other things, give Dawn more time to repair the tepee skin.

Chapter Eleven
~ The Lone Soldier ~

Come nightfall I shed my clothes, and, without bothering Dawn for the pelt bags, I decided to change into a wolf. Just as suddenly, I was on all fours looking down at my large, powerful wolf paws.

With some dinner in mind, I charged off into the great plains of Colorado, looking forward to the fun of the frolic and the hunt for food.

I wasn't having a good night's hunting when I ran into a clearing and found myself facing a pack of wolves. Considering I was interrupting their dinner of bison, they were not happy to see me. In fact, I believe the pack of four males and two females was getting ready to attack their dinnertime intruder—the intruder being me.

They were moving slowly from their dinner and looked as if they planned to encircle me ... until I decided to try to even the odds by changing into a large, angry grizzly with an attitude. The biggest of the four, who was straight in front of me, froze. The others followed their leader's example and stood their ground.

I stepped forward with a mighty roar and the pack, minus the leader, turned almost as one and ran, giving ground and their dinner to the mighty bear. The leader of the pack was a different story. I could see in his anger-filled eyes the reluctance to lose his dinner to me, and with a defiant growl, he suddenly made his move. To my surprise, he made no move to attack but rather turned and followed the rest of the pack, leaving me alone with a nice juicy bison for dinner. That bison was as fine as cream gravy.

I was still enjoying my stolen bison dinner when I heard screams echoing off in the distance, screams of severe, torturous pain. Screams violently forced from some poor wretch.

Out here, such torturous screams from a human could only mean Indians. I could not continue enjoying my bison dinner, knowing a human was being tortured and to such a degree as to create those screams. I'd be hearing them in my nightmares.

Believing my fastest form to be the coyote, I changed and charged off into the night, in the direction of those hellish screams. I'd probably traveled miles in minutes when I started smelling a campfire, and then sweat and fear. Slowing my pace considerably, I crept in closer to recon the situation without being spotted.

For the sake of cover, I moved to place a tree between the torture scene and me. It had been some time since I'd heard any screams. That meant the victim either had passed out from the pain or had blessedly died from shock and blood loss. There had been a considerable amount of blood loss at some point. The smell was almost overwhelming. From what I had heard of Indians and their ability to keep their victims alive for days, I figured this victim had most likely passed out, which meant the tortures of the damned would most likely recommence once the victim revived.

Keeping the tree in front of me, I sneaked closer to the encampment. As I reached the tree, I discovered a large branch that would probably hold my weight, so I jumped for it and landed with the silence of padded cat's paws.

What I found was a scene from hell. Two Indians were at the campfire, pointing and laughing at their handiwork. A naked man was hanging off a large branch, tied in place with parts of his intestines. I could see a deep cut that ran from hip to hip, with even more of his liver hanging out. I could see deep cuts from his groin to his knees, and the insides of both legs were still bleeding profusely. That told me the victim was still alive, if only barely. The lack of screams must have meant the poor wretch had passed out from his pain.

Even so, I couldn't believe the poor victim still lived, when an audible groan could be heard slipping from his lips, a groan that caught the attention of his torturers.

One Indian jovially said something to his companion in his native tongue while playfully hitting the other on the arm, and then got up to approach the damned. He was passing right under me, laughing and removing his knife from its sheath when I quickly and quietly changed into my larger, heavier wolf form and pounced on the Indian's back.

I hit him in the back with claws fully extended, so that they would dig into my damnable victim. As we hit the ground together, the impact forced my claws from his back, ripping out skin, muscle, and sinew as my prey and I separated. Now it was the Indian doing the screaming. I paused to enjoy the sight of him unsuccessfully trying to rise. Unsuccessful because of the pain and damage my mighty claws had done to his back.

A war whoop interrupted my enjoyment, as the other Indian was coming right for me on his charging pony. This deadly vision from hell was waving a war ax over his head with the intent of cleaving my head from the rest of my body.

I had other ideas.

I easily jumped and rolled to the side, avoiding both pony hooves and swinging war tool of death. Failing on his first attempt, the Indian brought his pony to an abrupt turn that brought it up on its hind legs. Once turned to face his foe, he momentarily froze at the sight of a very large grizzly bear roaring out where moments ago a wolf had been under attack.

Not to be outdone, the Indian let out a war whoop that failed to match my roaring anger, kicked his horse into action, and charged. As the war pony with the crazed eyes raced toward me, and his master attempted to bring the war ax down on my head, I grabbed the arm, which held the war ax and ripped it from the rest of the Indian. This action had two results. First, I had the Indian's war ax, arm and all, and second, the Indian, now screaming in pain, had been pulled from his pony. The pony, not such a fool as his rider, left his screaming, crazed master in the dirt as it kept going, wanting to be anywhere but around an angry grizzly that might, if given the chance, eat him.

The Indian, for the rest of his very short life, would be known as lefty. He tried to rise from the ground, so I walked over on my hind legs, to show off my entire eight-to-nine foot tall mass of furry fury when standing upright. Indians weren't the only ones who could put on a horror show to their enemies. Before this torturer of white men died, I was going to give him something to fear.

In one long, deep strike of my powerful paws, I ripped out the Indian's upper thigh muscles and sinews, leaving the Indian crippled, screaming, but alive to enjoy some of the pain he had found so much fun inflicting on his white captive. I then walked over to the other Indian, who had almost succeeded in getting up, and crippled him like I had his companion, ripping out his leg muscles with one strike of my power-filled paws. Now the two screamed in unison, and it wasn't war whoops they were a-screaming.

I figured I'd leave them alive to endure the mighty pain they so enjoyed inflicting on others. I also figured that eventually the smell of decay and blood would bring out the carnivorous creatures that might enjoy eating the crippled, defenseless Indians alive, like that pack of wolves I had stolen the bison dinner from.

Having taken care of the Indians to my pleasure, I changed back into my human form to look to the white captive. I gave no concern for my lack of clothes, but did pick up the Indian's knife for the purpose of cutting down the white man.

When I approached him, I was surprised to see he was still alive, through barely. He lifted his face slightly to me, and he pointed to a cache of items near the fire. He tried to say something, but only a light gurgle came from his massively bruised and extremely puffed-up face and lips.

I cut loose one hand and again he weakly pointed toward the cache of items that I couldn't see clearly from my position. While looking back to him, saying, "Something is sure import ..." I saw that the man was dead.

I cut loose his other arm and gently laid him down. Performing a recon of the area, I discovered the cache of items that was so important to the soldier, for a soldier he was. The cache of items included his uniform, and more importantly, a message pouch. I opened the pouch, and by firelight, I was able to see that the papers were for Capt. Edward Ball, Fort Wallace, Kansas. Being retired, I made a point of not reading the papers important enough to die for.

I found a horse blanket and rolled the remains of the soldier, as well as his equipment and uniform, into the blanket. During the battle, the second pony had made his escape, so I had no way of getting the soldier's remains back to our encampment. Looking the area over, I found there was a place where two strong-looking branches were near each other. This gave me the idea of placing the soldier's remains up off the ground, hopefully high enough to keep him from predators until I could return.

With the camp prepared as much as possible, I changed to coyote form and, just in case I couldn't find my way back, I grabbed up the message pouch in my jaws and made for home.

When I arrived at our encampment, I found Dawn sitting up, bow and arrows in easy reach. I filled her in on the evening's adventure. I placed the message pouch in Horse's saddlebag for safekeeping and for easy reach when needed.

Come the morning, we made for the Indian camp of torture with me in the lead. Within hours, I came to a place I recognized as being near our goal.

Thinking of the way I had left the Indians to be some nightly critters' fine dining, I turned back and halted Dawn's progress. "I suggest you stay here. I'll go on into the camp for the soldier's remains." She just nodded.

Arriving at the camp, I couldn't help but smile at the obvious signs that the two Indians I had left crippled, helpless, and alive had been dinner for some lucky critters. The wolf pack came to mind. While the Indians had definitely been eaten, I could see from my perch on Horse's back that the soldier's remains had not been disturbed.

I walked Horse up to the remains of the two Indians for a closer look. While this might seem a bit morbid, the corpses were right on the way to the soldier's remains and it's always a good idea to make sure that the dead are dead and not faking it so the supposed dead can bushwhack you in the back.

One Indian showed on his face the look of extreme pain he had been enduring when whatever carnivore had come to eat what was left of his back, legs, and arms. The other Indian didn't even have a face. He too was well eaten. I looked around and noticed the arm my grizzly self had removed and tossed away was gone. Some critter had run off with the dismembered arm to be eaten at its leisure.

I walked Horse up to the soldier's remains, blanket roll and all, and eased the blanket roll casket down and across the saddle horn in front of me. Horse was uneasy about carrying the dead, but followed orders and took me back to Dawn and the wagon. At the wagon, I carefully dismounted so as not to disturb the blanket roll until I was ready. From beside Horse, I reverently moved the blanket roll from over Horse's back to the back of the wagon.

"Now what do?" Dawn asked in a slight reverent tone.

"We head east, for Fort Wallace. There, we deliver these messages and this young soldier.

We hadn't traveled a day when I spied smoke in the distance, a long trail of black smoke. We picked up the pace and within hours, I spotted, off in the distance, the source of the smoke. It looked like a burned-out circle of a wagon train.

I charged ahead. There might still be living people among those ruins, and, if there were, they most likely would be in very needy condition.

Coming upon the ruins, I pulled-up Horse to a canter, and found two dead outside the circle. I slowed Horse to a stroll as we moved inside the circle of ruined wagons and found lots of dead. I maneuvered Horse among the dead bodies, in the hopes of finding someone, anyone, still alive. Mostly I found naked bodies with some men face down and some men face up. All the men were scalped. I was coming to the realization that all I was finding were men when Dawn pulled the wagon up just outside the circle and entered on foot. I observed her entering near one wagon, destroyed but not burned.

Dawn disappeared within the shadow of the wagon and was not there long when she called out. "Captain Cody, one live."

I jumped off Horse and ran over. Within the shadow, Dawn had the head of a young man lying in her lap, a young man who was not only still alive, but still had his clothes on. I noticed that where his scalp should have been was a dark brown crust of dried blood. I heard him say something that I could not hear from my standing position and quickly moved to his side.

He spoke in a weakened tone. "… They took my wife and two daughters. … I tried to stop th …"

Dawn looked to me. "He live, not long."

I ordered, "See to him," and added, after looking around, "and I'll see to the dead."

I started picking up dead men and stacking them like cords of wood into a wagon that hadn't been totally burned and was conveniently distant from the rest. I was shocked when I turned over the first dead man that was lying face down and discovered his genitals were hacked off and stuffed in the dead man's mouth. All those face down dead were in the same condition, with the exception of one who was found with a spear jammed up his hindquarters. He was hard to turn over, but with fortitude, I did finally succeed, getting him turned over to discover that the spear tip had been forced through the corpse's chest and apparently had the dead man tacked hard to the ground.

While completing my unpleasant task, I stole a burning branch from a cook fire Dawn had going and torched the wagon of the dead.

After seeing to Horse and the wagon's horse, I returned to the cook fire, where Dawn was busy fixing something to eat. As tired and disheartened as I was, it looked like a meal of vegetables for me, as I was just too tired to go hunting in beast form tonight.

I planted myself on a log. "What was with the dead Indian?
Bodies, some face up, some face down and mutilated."

Dawn concentrated on fixing dinner. "Ones face down enemy died coward. Ran from battle or killed self. Not take alive."

I recalled seeing wounds on those I turned over that looked self-inflicted.

"Ones laying face up died like warrior in battle, worthy to see journey to great beyond."

"The one we found still alive? He is still alive, isn't he?"

"He live. Rests. Left for dead, great warrior honor left."

"They didn't bother to leave him his scalp." I remembered a burned-up doll I had spotted by one of the dead men. "What of the women and children?"

"The Cheyenne take back to lodges and make part of tribe. They well treated. Captured young boys be Cheyenne warriors. Young women taught Indians ways by tribal women. Young girls—women, in Cheyenne way. Any who reach adulthood and fail to take the Cheyenne life allowed to leave."

The last surprised me. "The Cheyenne will just let them leave, just like that?"

"Cheyenne no kill just to kill," Dawn responded.

"Damn it. Why must there be all this killing? Is this land not big enough for both whites and Indians?" The latter I just about screamed in frustration.

Dawn stopped her cooking and looked straight at me. "Captain Cody, you travel great plains for many moons. See many buffalo?"

"Some..."

"Some. In time of Grandfather, we see herds of buffalo. Cannot count. See herds of buffalo and travel next to for two moons and never see beginning of herd or end of herd. In time of Grandfather, the Great

Plains trembled when mighty buffalo herd moved." I had never seen such feeling from her before.

"Why white men kill Buffalo?"

"To feed—"

She interrupted me. "Feed blue coats here to make treaties with the Indians. Then break treaties when not steal Indian land fast enough. White man kill buffalo to feed layers of steel rods laid across traditional buffalo hunting grounds, for loud iron beast move many white across buffalo hunting lands. White man kill buffalo and leave on ground," she spat out.

With feeling, she continued. "White man kill buffalo. Move on to kill more buffalo. As long as buffalo on plains, Indians killed buffalo with reverence. Use buffalo skins to warm families warm in hard winters. Use buffalo meat to feed families now and live through harsh winters. They use buffalo bones." As proof, from a bag she kept close, she removed the long bone tools I have often seen her use in repairing her tepee.

Replacing her tools, she continued. "Grandfather say white man kill buffalo to kill those who use lands white man want. Grandfather say, "Kill off buffalo, and kill off white man's enemy, Indians.'

"Why we kill bufalo? To preserve way of life. To live as our grandfathers and their grandfathers lived. To live on as Indian and not as white man want us live, as civilized white man and on handouts, planted on lands no one want or able live on."

The rest of the night passed quietly and uneventfully. By morning, I had one more dead man to plant.

We found our way onto the Santa Fe Trail and headed east, with our goal to find Fort Wallace, which would be somewhere on the trail just for those heading West. We were headed for Kansas. I would not have seen that in my stars.

The war and the end of fighting had ended only months before with the surrender of General Robert E. Lee on May 9, 1865. In November of the same year, word came to me that the Confederate guerrilla leader by the name William Clarke Quantrill had smashed through Kansas like a swarm of locusts. While there, he had killed off my family and burned down the family farm. While I looked forward to looking up the gentleman and introducing him to my saber, I later learned some Union forces had ambushed him in Kentucky soon after his visit to Kansas.

They robbed me and my saber of my revenge. I would have thought visiting Kansas would never hold anything for me.

We were on the great wide plains, with beautiful mountain ranges in the distance behind us, and more mountains to our distant left. All was quiet and tranquil, when Dawn let out an owl hoot to get my attention because Horse and I were traveling a short distance ahead of the wagon. I casually looked behind me and discovered Dawn pointing to the hills to our left. Turning in the saddle to look off to the left, I discovered what Dawn had seen. White smoke came from the hilltop. This was not an innocent white, puffy cloud, peacefully wafting in the blue skies. This was an Indian signal smoke, and could be big trouble.

I turned Horse around and trotted back to the wagon. After traveling slightly past the wagon, I turned Horse around again and walked him to Dawn's side.

"Think it's trouble?"

Looking around, she stopped searching. "Yes."

Glancing behind us, I saw the reason for her answer. Behind us was a distant cloud of dust and it wasn't a dust storm heading our way. It had to be riders, lots of riders, riding hard. Riding straight for us.

"Dawn, go. Travel hard."

I didn't have to say that twice. She slapped the wagon horse on its rump and let out a war whoop that scared the horse into racing for its life, not to mention ours.

Withdrawing my Sharps, I fell behind the wagon and, while keeping an eye behind us, trailed the wagon. Horse and I could easily outrun the wagon and Dawn and disappear in safety, but that wasn't a consideration.

It wasn't going to be hard for that dust storm of determined horsemen to catch us. Determined horsemen against a wagon meant the cards were not in our favor. I was fully aware of this. I just hoped we could come to some place where we could set up a defensive position and hope for the best. All I could see ahead of Dawn was a lot of open territory that wouldn't provide a good hiding place for a prairie rabbit.

We had no hope but to find some place to defend ourselves, because out here in the open we didn't stand a chance. At this point, it looked like we didn't have a chance anyway.

I had no way of knowing how many horsemen were tailing us, but it had to be too many for me to handle alone to be producing such a dust cloud behind us.

We traveled some distance when I pulled up and faced Horse into the direction of the oncoming storm, a storm of possibly a couple of dozen Indians charging after us. All I could see ahead of Dawn was a lot of open, indefensible territory. I took careful aim with the Sharps and dropped a heavily head-dressed Indian, and they just kept coming.

I placed the spent Sharps back into its scabbard and pulled out my Henry repeater. If these Indians were not familiar with the repeater rifle, they were in for an unpleasant surprise.

I dropped to my feet and gave Horse a slap on the ass to get him out of the battlefield. "Go, old friend," I said because it looked like I most likely would not be seeing him again. The Indians charged ahead, whooping and yelling, waving spears, bows, and old-style rifles over their heads. Whooping and yelling at the sight of such an easy kill, they just kept on coming.

I assumed the kneeling position, raised the Henry to my shoulder, took aim, and started dropping Indians. They still came on, yelling and carrying on at the thought of what ease one white man was going to be. I just kept firing. I noticed one Indian drop backward off his horse after I got him in the chest. It appeared that the Indian had been tied to his horse's reins. Now the dead or dying Indian was being dragged by his frightened horse, which was causing some confusion among the horsemen behind him.

Making full use of my repeater, I just kept dropping Indians as they kept coming. Suddenly, a sharp, burning pain in the front of my leg distracted me. Looking down, I discovered an arrow protruding from it. Distracted by the offensive protrusion, another hit me in the upper right arm, causing me to drop my rifle.

* * * *

To my surprise, I was feeling déjà vu as I found myself slowly waking in Dawn's tepee. I was pulled fully awake by pain as I started to move my arm while in the act of getting into a sitting position.

"Please, Captain Cody, lay quiet. All well."

My voice was dry and rough, but I had to ask, "How is it … how is it I am still alive?"

"You face war party of Cheyenne. One brave man against many

braves."

"So how is it … I'm still living?"

"I watch you defend us. You fight like strong brave. Too many warriors. You flinch, drop weapon. I see end for us."

"What happened?" I mustered an order in my voice.

"You change to great Grizzly Bear. You pull arrows from leg, arm with fierce growl. You charge war party. War party to last warrior turn ponies, and ride. Race away. No fight angry Grizzly Bear.

"When change, Captain Cody, injuries make pass out. I pitch camp. Treat injuries. You be fine. Need rest. Clothes not good."

I realized I was naked under a large animal pelt, with wrappings around my arm and leg. Thinking it over, the best I could figure was that I must have lost my temper in a moment of desperation, and out of total frustration accidentally changed into my grizzly bear form. Bully for you, Cody O'Conner, I congratulated myself.

After a few days of veggie meals, I recovered enough to go out nights in my beastly forms. The changes in physical form may have hastened my recovery because I recovered in record time.

After a week, we broke camp and continued on our way to Fort Wallace. During that time, Horse returned, I totally healed, and the soldier in the wagon got quite potent. Dawn came up with some strong-smelling wild flowers that kept the dead bearable. During that week, we were not disturbed by man, Indian, or beast.

.

Chapter Twelve
~ Somewhere in Kansas ~

Finally, we made it to Fort Wallace, or what there was of it. Fort Wallace was still under construction. The fortifications weren't even complete. The fort wall did encompass the fort, but came up short in the front, hence no front gate, just an unusually wide entryway.

I could easily see right onto the parade ground, a parade ground busy with men holding horses and even more men riding horses. A cavalry outpost.

Looking on, I saw one large building past the parade ground, which I assumed was the headquarters, and to the side and further back was a tent town I supposed was the soldier quarters. Off in a corner were more buildings with some fencing that appeared to be stables for all the soldiers' horses.

When Dawn caught up with me with the wagon, we moved forward toward Fort Wallace together.

As we neared the gateway, a small group of soldiers halted our progress. "Halt and state your business."

"Captain Cody O'Conner, Second Regimental Cavalry, Kansas City, retired. I came upon a soldier some days back, and I have dispatches for a General George Armstrong Custer. Who's in command here, and where can I find him?"

"Those dispatches would be for the commander of this here Fort Wallace, General George Armstrong Custer of the U.S. Seventh Calvary." This he announced with pride, but I noted his attention change as he took to looking over Dawn.

"She's with me, private," I snapped, using my best commanding voice.

"Ah, yes Sir. Just take your wagon and yourself over to that big building on the far side of the parade grounds. Someone there will assist you, Sir."

Following directions landed me in front of the Headquarters, where more soldiers met us. The ranking officer greeted me. "You have business here, Sir?"

"I have a dead soldier in the back of this wagon I would be mighty glad to be rid of. I also have official dispatches I found with the soldier's belongings. His last request was for me to deliver them."

The Lieutenant turned and pointed to two soldiers standing near. "You and you remove said dead soldier from this wagon and take him over to the infirmary. If nothing else, search his belongings to find his name, rank, and where he was stationed."

He turned back to me. "I'm assuming that official messenger pouch you are carrying has the dispatches in them. Please come with me, and I'll see if the commander can see you now."

We entered the outer office. "Please wait here. Who may I say wishes to see the Commander?"

"With his pleasure, Captain Cody O'Conner, Second Regimental Cavalry, Kansas City, retired."

With that, he turned, militarily crisp, knocked on the door, and with proper military hesitation, opened the door respectfully and entered. A couple of minutes later, he opened the door for me and bid me enter.

Upon entering, I found a gentleman, youngish looking for a commander, busy with some papers. I couldn't help but notice his long, golden, wavy hair, which came with a full blond mustache and beard. He had a head of hair any Indian warrior would be proud to have on his spear. I couldn't help but hope that he was going to be able to keep it.

Finally, he gave attention to me. "I have been made to understand you have something for me?"

Stepping forward, displaying my military training, I handed him the message bag.

"Please, Captain O'Conner, retired. Have a seat and give me a moment of your time after I quickly peruse these papers you have been so nice to deliver."

While he read the documents over, I did as instructed. Finally, he placed the papers down in front of him. "I understand you got these from a dying soldier. Please give me the details."

I told him how I had followed the sounds of screams and come upon an Indian encampment where two Indians were torturing a soldier. Of course, I changed the facts a little, giving the impression that I had come across the camp in human form and in such form had dispatched the Indian torturers.

He listened intently and didn't interrupt my rendition with any questions. After I finished, he got up from his desk and faced a large wall map. "You wouldn't mind coming over here and showing me about where you found this unfortunate soldier?"

After walking up to the map, I easily spotted where someone had written on it "Fort Wallace" and followed my finger a little northwest from there. Trying to judge our journey, I picked a likely spot. "I'd guess about here, Sir."

"First off, the area you're pointing to indicates you were already in Kansas when you found the Indian encampment. Secondly, I just came back from patrolling that area, say about the time you were there. I was out searching for a patrol of mine that hadn't arrived when expected.

"My patrol did indeed find our missing Lt. Kitter and his patrol all murdered. Expected dispatches were not found on or around him. My guess would be that Lt. Kitter, finding himself and his men outnumbered, had one soldier sneak away with the dispatches, and the ploy wasn't totally successful. While I can't share the importance of those dispatches with you, I can say you served your country well in getting them to me. Please have a seat and allow me a minute of your time."

After we both were seated, he spoke again. "By any chance would you be looking for a job?"

"Sorry, General, but you have as much of a chance of getting me to re-enlist as you would getting Red Cloud to enlist."

"No, I wasn't going to ask you to enlist. You could serve this fort well, and get paid doing it. I'm in bad need of a buffalo hunter. What fort cattle the local Indians haven't stolen from us, they have killed off. Winter's not far off, and we already are having food problems."

"Sorry again, General, but a large salary is no good to a dead man. Buffalo hunting in this area right now would be suicide, and I have plans to keep my scalp, if you please."

"I was told you arrived with an Indian woman riding with you. I thought maybe you had it in with the local Indians, possibly through marriage?"

70

"She's Navajo, General. The Sioux and Cheyenne would just as soon kill her as they would me."

"I see, in that case I'd suggest you continue heading east from here, as this is not a safe area for any white man right now."

"I'll strongly consider that, Sir. If I may suggest: just don't you get yourself in any Indian trouble you can't get out of, Sir."

With that, he picked up some papers and got busy looking at them. I took that as my cue that I was dismissed.

In the outer office, I addressed the officer in command. "Captain?"

"Captain Bankhead, at your service."

"Captain Bankhead, any problem with me bunking here for the night and setting out in the early morn?"

"No problem for yourself, Sir, but I strongly advise against ..."

"My traveling companion?"

"Sir, no offense, but we can put you up in the bachelor quarters with the civilians working to build this here Fort Wallace, but we have no facilities for a single female, and, quite frankly, I wouldn't suggest leaving her alone around here. We have had a lot of unpleasant activities with the local redskins and there are a lot of injured feelings among the troops."

"I get the point, Captain. Thank you."

When I came out, I found Dawn faithfully waiting for me by the wagon, in the intense summer heat. "Dawn, I'm going to spend the night here in the fort. I don't like it, but you are going to have to pitch camp outside. I suggest close by the fort. Return here at sunrise, and we'll start out in the morning."

"Where?"

"Possibly south to find a place and a job to winter. At this point, I'm not sure."

With Dawn heading out the fort entrance, I took Horse to the stables for the night. Afterward, I went to the camp latrine. It was just a large pit with lumber walls for some privacy. At least it was a pit I hadn't had to dig, use, and later fill in before hitting the trail.

Dinner in the mess hall was edible, but don't ask me what it was. Dinner made me feel a little guilty for turning the General down on his job offer as a buffalo hunter. Afterward, I found me an empty bunk at the bachelors' quarters, which wasn't difficult to find, as it was only one of two wooden-walled, roofed structures currently existing, not including the HQ building. I guessed the other was officer territory. I even heard complaints from the camp surgeon over the fact that the hospital didn't even have a roof as of yet, but at least he wasn't working out of a walled tent.

Come the morning, I awoke to the sounds of other civilians and soldiers getting ready for the new day.

Even though it was hours before the sun would be getting out of bed, I had no trouble getting up and getting ready to face the day. After all, I had grown up on a farm, and went from farming to soldiering, so getting up early was my routine.

I then checked Horse, seeing to his breakfast so he had time to eat while I got some grub. The mess hall, which had been lit up like a prairie fire for hours already, was already busy feeding the troops, civilian workers, and soldier alike. Desperation must have been the reason for the busy hour, as the food could not have been the reason. After getting my fill of some mystery mess, I got back to Horse.

As I entered the stables, Horse greeted me with a nod and a kicking of his front legs, telling me let's get me dressed and going. Walking Horse to the parade grounds, I headed toward the HQ. From the light of the building, I could see Dawn sitting stalwartly in the wagon seat, waiting for my arrival. Looking toward the east, I could just see the sun getting out of bed to face the day and was preparing a heavily warm day for both man and beast.

I knew Dawn heard me coming, but she just sat there on the wagon bench seat as if she had not. "Mornin, Dawn. Have any trouble getting back inside the fort?"

"Tell blue coats I with Captain O'Conner. Tell blue coats Captain O'Conner was friend of Yellow Hair. They let me in."

I swung into the saddle. "Let's head east some and get out of Indian-troubled area."

Just then, Captain Bankhead came marching out of the HQ with a purposeful stride, straight for us. "Mr. O'Conner, General Custer would like your presence in his office. Please, sir."

That "Please, sir' cinched it. This wasn't a casual invitation. So I dismounted and followed Captain Bankhead into the General's office.

There, I found the young General looking quite a bit older than he had just the day before. With him was an older man I wasn't acquainted with, but it wasn't hard to figure him for an Indian scout.

On my entrance, both the General and his guest turned from the large, crude wall map and looked my way. The general started the introductions. "Captain O'Conner, retired, this is Mitch Bouyer. He's been working for me. Mitch, please fill O'Conner in about the situation."

"I was on the Santa Fe Trail bound for here, coming from Fort Riley. I left some hours after a stage had left, so much later than the stage that I never figured to see it until I got here, if at all. Halfway between Fort Riley and here, I came on the remains of the stage. The horses had all been killed by arrows. The driver, shotgun rider, and two male passengers were first shot and then arrowed. The cash box was missing."

"Cheyenne or Sioux?" I interjected.

"Sioux arrows were all over the place," Mitch answered, "but it was no injun attack. Sioux wouldn't kill off the horses. They would have taken them. Close examination showed the men had been shot down with .44s and then arrowed. My people would have no use for the cash box. No, this was done by a well-trained gang of white men. Tracks showed a group of shod horses had attacked the stage, then charged off to the north—"

This time the General interrupted. "What Mitch Bouyer hasn't told you is that my wife was on that stage. Whoever the gang was, they took my wife with them. Sir, I would like you to go after that gang and, by any means possible, bring back my wife to me. I would do it myself in a heartbeat, but I have no authority in Nebraska, and you can bet that's where that gang can be found."

Seeing the pain in the General's face, I could not do anything but agree to go after his wife. "I'll start out right now."

"Is there anything I can supply you with … weapons, horses, anything?"

Giving it some thought, I realized I was well supplied with everything but foodstuff, and, after eating in the camp mess hall, I knew the General couldn't help me there. "No, I'm fully supplied."

"Good hunting, then. One thing, I'm going to Fort Riley myself to see if there is anything I can find out from there. If the gang is going to leave a ransom note, they would most likely leave it at Fort Riley."

"Unless there is anything else, I'll hit the trail after those 'wife thieves.'"

Heading out, I traveled alongside Dawn, filling her in on our new quest.

Her only response was, "Where you go, I go."

Chapter Thirteen
~ After the General's Wife ~

So, we traveled the Santa Fe Trail eastward until we came across the doomed stagecoach. From there, I found the trail of horse tracks Mitch Bouyer had mentioned that he found heading north. We followed that trail until night was coming on, and then we quit for the night. My guess was if we were not already in Nebraska, we were close to it.

I spent some of the night quenching my desire for some fresh meat with some venison I killed in wolf form. After dining at Fort Wallace, I have to say the venison was a breath of fresh air, like after leaving the camp latrine.

The next day, we came across a cold campsite, likely where the gang had held up for the night. The camp not only held the right number of horses but I also found the stage cash box, shot open and empty. What was surprising was the tracks leaving the campsite. The tracks went on a heading of southeast. Then it hit me like a right cross, Fort Riley was southeast of here. The gang was heading for Fort Riley to supply a ransom note.

After spending the morning searching the cold camp for clues, we took a nooner, and then we continued following the tracks. Two days later, we lost the tracks to some hard rocky ground, but during our tracking, the trail the gang was putting down never varied from their southeast heading, land obstacles aside. I fully suspected the gang was heading for Fort Riley to deliver a ransom note.

Eventually, we arrived at Fort Riley and to a wagon train full of surprises.

The front gate gave me directions to the HQ, which was very helpful, as Fort Riley was a large, fully functioning fort made up of many stone buildings. Quite the change from Fort Wallace.

Within the HQ, I was introduced to the commander, Colonel Andrew J. Smith. He handed me my next surprise.

"Sorry, but I can't allow you to visit General Custer, as he is under arrest for abandoning his post when he came here."

"You realize why General Custer is here?" I barely held back my frustration and anger.

"I am fully informed of the situation. I am also fully instructed in military law. General in Chief of the U.S. Army, Ulysses S. Grant, has ordered this court-martial. I may also have some useful information for you."

On cue, a fellow stepped forth from a corner shadow. "This is Wild Bill Hickok, Army Scout. He's a friend of General Custer, and, as a scout, knows this area well."

I shook hands with him. "Has a ransom note been received for Mrs. Custer?"

"Not as yet," the colonel in charge answered. "We have been expecting one, but as yet we have heard nothing."

"Strange, I followed a trail of horses leaving the stagecoach heading north, then after camping and shooting open the cash box, they were heading this way when I lost their trail. I assumed the gang was heading here to deliver a ransom note in some way."

"Well, as of yet, none has arrived to our attention. The front gate has orders to deliver any strange messages or letters to us immediately."

"I may possibly have some helpful information," Wild Bill interjected.

"Just call me Cody," I said, filling in his pause.

"Southwest of here is an abandoned fort that in its time had many names, the last being Fort Atkinson. It was retired years ago, when the Oregon Trail was replaced by the Santa Fe Trail. It's an impenetrable stone fortress. Sometimes the place has been used by the occasional passerby, but no more. Word has it that a gang that shoots first and doesn't bother to ask questions of dead intruders is using the fortress. I believe a rebel Confederate gang is holed up in there. Stealing horses, robbing stagecoaches, murdering, and making it look like the Indians did it has definitely been their style."

"But whoever hit the stage killed the horses," I interrupted.

"We have been fully briefed. Mitch Bouyer left Fort Riley hours afterward. He may have interrupted them and shortened their plans."

"If it's known that this Confederate gang terrorizing the area is holed up in this fort, why hasn't anyone gone in and cleaned them out?"

"The old fort is an impenetrable fortress with a canyon on three sides."

"It looks like this fort is my next stop," I said.

"Figured you'd say that, so I drew up a map to help you find the place. I'd go with you, but the army here has got other plans for me."

The Commander, Colonel Andrew J. Smith, interrupted, "How do you plan on getting in and getting Mrs. Custer out without getting the both of you killed?"

Taking the map, I turned my attention to the Commander. "I have learned some tricks that will come in handy, believe me. I have no plans on getting either Mrs. Custer or myself killed."

Dawn and I left camp without incident. We traveled southwest, following the map so carefully made for me. I kept a keen eye out for Indians, and Dawn was even quieter than usual.

One night after setting up camp, I changed into wolf form with the idea of getting me some fresh meat for dinner. I'd been patrolling the area for some hours when I heard voices, voices speaking in some Indian lingo.

I moved stealthily toward the voices, making sure not to step on a twig or dry branch that might snap and give away my location. Despite being in the dark, I made a point of approaching low to the ground, using any little brush I could find for concealment.

Eventually, I got close enough to confirm an Indian raiding party of about a dozen or more. As was typical, they had no guards out for me to worry about. I had learned that Indians—either from arrogance or because they believe no one attacks at night, since Indians don't by nature—never bother putting out guards at night.

Concerned with their possible closeness to Dawn's camp, I slunk off into the night. After putting distance between their camp and myself, I charged off to warn Dawn for the need to move camp.

Dawn had other ideas. She explained while hunting through the bag of pelts, "We not move camp. We change medicine and force them to move camp."

"Mind explaining that?"

She continued hunting through the pelt bag. "They not wander close to settlements and forts unless they believed their medicine good." Her difficulty in finding what she was looking for was beginning to distract her explanation.

I grabbed her hand from the pelt bag. "What are you looking for?"

"I look for animal you have not changed to yet. I look for winged belt of wise old owl."

"For now, just explain why you're looking for his belt."

"Apaches and Cheyenne believe owl bad medicine. Owl sign of death. If you fly over encampment, fly close, Indians may fear medicine gone bad, break camp, leave area."

Thinking of a barn owl that used to inhabit my parents' barn, I suddenly found my vision even stronger, but a lot lower.

"Yes," Dawn exclaimed.

I flew off in the direction of the Indian camp and, making a point of flying between them and the near full moon, I flew a circle around the camp, screaming like one crazed harbinger of death.

When I observed the Indians jumping to their feet and pointing my way, I knew I had their attention. I flew in closer, making a point of almost bombarding the Indians, who reacted by starting to scream unintelligibly.

Having made my intentions clear, I flew off to a nearby dried-out tree; it provided a limb for me to land on. There, I watched as the Indians broke camp and quickly headed out of the area, haunted by the crazed, notorious harbinger of death.

Their medicine had definitely gone bad.

The next day, we moved on without any interference from Indians. Eventually, we arrived at a river that the map indicated led from the mountain and from behind the fortress. I was willing to bet that the river ran either right next to the fortress or into the fortress to supply residents with constant water, even during a time of siege.

Even though we still had hours of daylight, I suggested we set up camp, as we were still a safe distance from the fort, but in easy flight range for my eagle nature. After we finished setting up camp, and the horses were all taken care of, I figured it was time to challenge Dawn's silence.

"So, you going to tell me what's bothering you?"

Giving me her hardest stare, she responded, "YOU take on fortress of evil ones alone? You Skin-walker, not immortal."

"I forgot nothing. First, I plan to recon the fortress area from overhead in my eagle form. I will endeavor to gain as much information as I can on the layout, the number of 'evil ones' present, their locations, and the location and condition of Mrs. Custer. I will then fly back here to figure out a plan. If I feel it's possible to get Mrs. Custer and myself out of the fortress with as little fuss and danger as possible, I will. If it looks impossible … well let's wait and see. Remember, I'm not here to put Mrs. Custer in danger. I have some experience in recon and planning strategic maneuvers"

"No understand stra … tegic man … euvers?" she interrupted.

"I mean, I learned a few things fighting a four-year war that I was too young and stupid to not get involved in." I didn't bother to add anything about how many men died following my strategic maneuvers.

"No get killed attacking a … fortress of evil ones by self. Blue coat leader say army no get in fortress."

"The blue coat leader did not say many blue coats couldn't get inside. He said an army could not get inside without getting Mrs. Custer killed. However, just maybe a single Skin-walker can. We'll see tonight."

Chapter Fourteen
~ The Impenetrable Fortress ~

Come nightfall, in eagle form, I flew in the direction of the mountains and the impenetrable fortress. I followed the river, which eventually took me almost right to the front gate.

From my high vantage point, I viewed the general layout of the fortress. Built in a canyon with high, steep mountainous walls on three sides, the fort had a high gate of timbered logs at the one and only entrance. There were two guards, one on top of each fortified wall, stationed on either side of the large front gate. Both were in Confederate uniforms. I don't mean confederate rags. They were both decked out in full uniform and both carried a quick-loading, multi-firing Spencer rifle.

Despite the late hour, there was still activity within the fortifications. I found a cliff edge to roost on and eagle-eyed the situation. The more I watched, the more concerned I became. This was not a bunch of desperados under the leadership of a money-hungry despot. No, by all appearances this was a trained unit of Confederate soldiers under the leadership of a commissioned officer of the CSA that obviously had refused to face the fact that the war was over.

The parade ground, while small, was spit-n-shine. The horse corral was clean of any sign of the usual use by horses. The fort's interior contained three buildings, all facing the parade ground. Behind the building that faced the parade grounds and also faced the front gate were the corral and stables, and in the distant corner was the latrine.

I continued to watch over things until the camp had shown for some time signs of being quiet for the night. I even observed the changing of the guards. Then, I made my move.

I flew down onto the center building, and continued to watch for signs of life on the grounds, but saw and heard none. After a while, I flew down onto the ground behind the building and changed into my wolf form. I considered my coyote form as being possibly a stealthier form, but the wolf form gave me easier access to the windows, and I wanted to have a look into the various buildings to see what I faced, as well as spy out Mrs. Custer's location. I snuck around to the side of the building and looked through the window to discover what appeared to be the commander's office.

Behind a large desk was a large wall map, framed on either side with a Confederate flag. The room was dimly lit, and it was easy to see why. In the corner by a door sat a soldier who, from his breathing, was resting on guard duty. Who could he possibly be guarding but Mrs. Custer? I took note of the Spencer rifle leaning against the wall next to him. It looked like this was a well-armed unit of soldiers, although possibly a little lax in military training. That guard sounded like he was sleeping on duty, even if only lightly.

I made my way around to the other side of the building and looked in a window. I judged my location to be on the other side of the door from where I had observed the sleeping guard. Within was a large bed filled with white quilts, pillows, and a head of golden hair—Mrs. Custer, I presumed. Now that I had found her, it would be a good idea to see what forces I faced.

I crept around to the back of the closest building and could easily hear a load of restful breathing and someone snoring like a two-man saw. Easing up to the window, I peered into the building and saw about seven sleeping forms. Apparently, this was the bunkhouse. These seven, the one on guard duty, and the two guarding the front gate so far made a unit of ten, and I still hadn't seen anyone that looked in command of this outfit.

I had one more building to check. I padded around behind the back to the center building, going slowly and staying up close to the building to avoid attracting the attention of the horses and scaring up unwanted, noisy attention by spooking them.

Coming up behind the back of the building that faced the sleeping quarters, I discovered lights and the smell of coffee. Two men in Confederate officer dress were looking over a map on a table between them.

The one in a junior officer uniform spoke. "I'm concerned about the late return of the two picked to deliver the ransom note. All they had to do was to ride up close enough to the fort to shoot an arrow into the grounds with the ransom note attached to it. They should not have been that far behind us."

"As I pointed out before," the senior officer replied, "we can't do anything about them now. Next week a herd of cattle will be coming up from Texas, heading for Fort Wallace. We'll need every man we have to head off that cattle drive and make sure it doesn't get to its destination. Currently, we've made the food problem so bad there that some of the soldiers are deserting, and those that aren't may still be at the fort because they're too sick to leave. We need to keep them hungry until Fort Wallace has no food left and has to close for good. Our plan to remove Custer from command is working so well, there's really no need to rush Mrs. Custer back to her husband, is there?"

"No, sir."

I had seen and heard enough. I moved away from the window so that when I changed back into eagle form and went flapping off, I would not be heard taking flight.

From the vantage of the cliff's edge, I had another look over the fortifications and discovered a small building some feet from the latrine and almost hidden within an enclave of the fort's mountain wall. I knew I'd better have a look, but its closeness to the stables gave me cause for concern. Eventually, I figured if I swooped in toward the building's roof while staying close to the mountain wall, there was a good chance I could get to the building without disturbing the horses.

Once I landed on the roof, I immediately discovered the overwhelming smell of gunpowder. Changing into human form, I swung down off the roof to land on my bare feet in front of a door. The door was barred, but not locked. I removed the bar quietly and ducked into the building. I was instantly glad I was able to see around the room with the moonlight coming in from the open door because the room was full of kegs of gun-power and racks of Spencer and Sharp rifles. I was still looking around when I heard footsteps approaching.

Not having time to leave the building, I eased the door nearly closed, painfully aware of the door not being barred. Whoever was approaching and looking this way might see that.

I was relieved when I observed, through the slightly opened doorway, a man walking by, heading for the latrine. He looked like one forced out of bed by nature, but not necessarily forced to a total state of awareness.

When he walked behind the latrine wall, I silently slipped out of the building and replaced the bar. I grabbed the lip of the building roof and pulled myself back onto the roof. There, I changed back into my eagle self and flew back to my cliffside observation post, leaving the call-of-nature soldier none the wiser. Not long after, I observed sleepyhead heading back to bed, and all was quiet again.

I flew back to Dawn, dressed, and got some sleep. Later I would make plans for the rescue of Mrs. Custer. For the moment, I had no idea how I was going to manage it.

One thing officering had taught me was when to put problems aside temporarily for the purpose of getting a well-needed rest.

The next day as the sun went to hiding behind the fortified mountain range, Dawn stirred the fire. "Captain Cody have plan save Mrs. Custer?"

"Yep, I'm going to wing it." With that, I morphed into my golden eagle physique, with my now oversized man clothes dropping to the ground around my claws. Once my wings were free, I took flight straight for the impenetrable fortress.

I flew practically right over the heads of the gate guards without either one even glancing up my way. I made a straight flight right to my favorite cliff perch for further recon of the fort's interior activities.

After a couple of hours, the fort quieted down for the night. Unlike the night before, even the officers hit the bunkhouse for the night. With all quiet, I flapped down to the ground and, in wolf physique, I slipped up to the window that had revealed the positioning of the door guard. I peeked inside. A guard was there, but not the same one from the night before. This one was awake and alert. This could be a problem.

I moved away from the window, to morph back into my eagle self and fly unobserved back to my observation point.

With all quiet, it was time for hell to break loose.

I took flight, circling upward until I reached an altitude that would allow me to drop like a missile from God, plunge right into the first of the two gate guards, and fly off with such speed the second guard wouldn't have a chance in hell of getting a shot at me. As I prepared for my attack, I noted both guards were looking outward and had their backs to me.

I dove in so fast and so sharply that the first guard never knew what had smashed into his back, hitting him so hard he barely had time to scream in surprise before he went plunging over the top of the lumbered fortifications to his death. When I hit him, I pushed off him and upward from the plunging body to regain altitude for another round. This time my target would be alert and looking for my attack.

I took aim from behind my target, but this time, after taking aim, and diving at my alert target, I let out a screech that turned him my way. Before he could raise his weapon to take aim at me, I plunged my outstretched claws right into his face. My claws ripped into his cheeks and cheekbones, while other claws popped his eyes like grapes playfully crushed in a youthful hand, a hand hunting for the grapes' juices.

In shocked reflex, he reached for the claws that were busily ripping out his face and eyes. He dropped his rifle without even firing a shot. He brought his hands up to my flesh-and-bone-ripping claws, grabbing at them. This only worsened the attack on him because I had to rip around his face and hands to keep my claws free from his probing, protesting fingers.

When I felt the fight going out of him, I flapped my powerful wings and flew a foot away from him. While falling toward the lumber, I quickly morphed into my wolf form and charged him, knocking him backward and over the fortifications. As he plunged to his death, screaming all the way, I jumped down to the ground and paused, listening for any sound of raised alarm. However, the thick fortifications had buffered the screams of both guards; no one heard anything within the fort except for one lone werewolf.

Hearing nothing but silence, except for one noisy snorer within the bunkhouse, I changed into my human form and pulled open one of the two large gates. With the gate door left open, it crossed my thoughts that a night call to the latrine could cause everything to go very wrong, but it was a chance I had to be take

Morphing back into my mighty wolf physique, I dodged off to the right, which quickly had me quietly moving behind the cookhouse and mess hall. Passing the structure in silence took me back up to the window that gave me the best view of Mrs. Custer's guard. While still awake, he showed signs of settling in for the night.

Morphing into my smaller coyote form, I slipped around toward the front of the building and waited for any sign of activity. All stayed quiet.

I sneaked onto the porch, staying as low as possible to stay as far from the porch lamps as I could. Near the entrance door, I froze yet again to sniff for any activity. When all proved quiet, I morphed into my man form and slowly eased open the door, leaving it ajar. Then, I changed into my wolf form, charged the door into the room, and pushed the door open and out of the way. I rushed up to the near-slumbering guard and clamped my frightful fangs into the guard's throat before he could even think of raising an alarm.

I allowed the newly dead soldier to slump to the floor and listened carefully for any sound of activity. I was rewarded with continual silence except for some distant snoring from the bunkhouse. No wonder no one heard my deadly activities.

Changing into human form, I donned the clothes of the dead soldier, bloodstains and all. I noted that the building had a back door and used it, silently, to gain entrance to the stables and a couple of horses which I quickly, but silently, saddled.

I walked the horses to the back of the building where Mrs. Custer slept, and tied them at the back door. Now, for Mrs. Custer. I quickly and silently slipped back into the building and up to the door leading to her. The door was not locked, so I slipped in and, like an Indian, slunk up to the sleeping Mrs. Custer. She slept on her back, so I clamped my hand over her mouth, which caused her eyes to pop open in alarm.

"Mrs. Custer," I whispered into her ear, "I'm here to rescue you."

With her eyes displaying less alarm, I removed my hand from her mouth. "Mrs. Custer, it's imperative you be as quiet as possible. I suggest you leave any talking to me. Follow me out the back of the building where I have two horses waiting. I have the front gate open, so we can walk the horses out the front gate. Silence is the key to our getting out of here alive. Do you understand?"

She just nodded her head. The lack of words from her spoke very loudly of both her understanding of our predicament and her understanding of my directions.

She silently followed me out the back of the building and to the horses. I handed one set of reins to her and showed her how to put one hand on the horse's snout to help impress on it that it should be calm and quiet. She followed my lead.

We quietly walked the horses around to the side of the structure that put us on the other side of the building from the bunkhouse. As we neared the parade grounds, I had her stop and wait while I checked all was still clear. It was, so we slowly and silently started out.

Then it happened.

I heard the bunkhouse door open.

I touched Mrs. Custer in a way that signaled her to follow me backwards, back to the side of the center building. I slipped up to the corner, waiting for someone to appear, find the gate open, find the guards missing, and raise an alarm that most likely would get Mrs. Custer and me killed.

A man in his long johns stepped from the building and sleepily turned in the general direction of the latrine. I observed the man lumbered along without even bothering to raise his head. Apparently he was well used to these nightly trips to the latrine, to the point of not even bothering to fully wake up.

I hand gestured for Mrs. Custer to stay put, while handing her the reins to my horse. I quickly, but quietly, moved back behind the building and to the far corner. Once in place, I pinned myself to the back of the building. The plan was: as sleepyhead walked by, I would reach out and quickly twist his neck until it snapped like a chicken being prepared for dinner. That was the plan.

As he started to pass me, and I started to make my move, he must have heard something that drove him instantly and alarmingly awake. He turned in my direction, popped his eyes open, and opened his mouth to take in a large lung full of air. The alarm in his eyes turned to shock, and then death doused it as I reached out and ripped his throat out with my wolf claws.

I don't know who was more surprised at what had just happened, him or me. I was still in human form, except for my wolf-like arms and claws. I had instantly, but only partially, changed from man to wolf-man. I'd be very interested to know if Dawn knew of this wolf-man configuration. Mrs. Custer. She mustn't see this. With that thought, my arms and hands visibly became human again.

Returning to Mrs. Custer's side, I gestured for us to walk the horses behind the cookhouse. I had noticed the bunkhouse door was still open. She followed, staying quiet and wordless. By way of the back of the cookhouse building, we made it unseen to within sight of the open gate.

Putting a hand on Mrs. Custer's shoulder, I whispered into her ear. "Walk your horse quietly out that open gate. After walking a few feet from the gate, get on the horse and trot out of the canyon. Then ride like the devil is at your back while keeping close to the river. Eventually you will come to an Indian woman on a wagon. Go with her. Is that clear? Just nod."

She nodded in the affirmative.

"If you hear any commotion or sounds of alarm before getting to the gate, jump on your horse and ride like the demons of hell are after you. Is that clear?"

She again nodded in the affirmative.

"I'll be covering your …" I whispered. "I'll be protecting you from behind. Don't be concerned if you don't see me. Don't look back for me. Now, quietly walk out the gate."

She followed my orders very well. It's possible being married to a General may have had something to do with it. As she eased toward the open gate, one hand under the horse's head and the other on its muzzle, she moved smoothly and calmly. I'm sure a lot more calmly than she was feeling. While I took an occasional glance her way to watch her progress, most of my attention was on that menacing open bunkhouse door. It had just occurred to me why it was so menacingly quiet. That excessive snoring had ceased at some point. This didn't bode well.

I left the horse, and with Spencer rifle in hand, I quietly moved to the other side of the mess/cookhouse. When I reached the side that faced the center building, I planted myself where I could continue to watch the bunkhouse. Leaning the rifle against the wall, I quickly shed my clothes by changing into eagle form. Once, like a snake sheds skin, I had shed my stolen clothes. I then morphed from eagle to wolf and continued to watch the bunkhouse. I sneaked past the building corner enough to watch the hindquarter of Mrs. Custer's horse being swallowed up by the black maw of the open gate door. A creak of a distant wood plank jerked my attention back to the bunkhouse. A large form was emerging.

The zombie-like form just continued walking out onto the porch and, without looking in any direction, just continued shuffling off the porch and straight for me and the mess/cookhouse.

I eased back a step, becoming one with the dark shadows of the building. The zombie kept coming, not noticing a thing amiss. As he neared the building, he glanced sideways in the general direction of the gate and froze.

As I faded back out of the protection of the shadows, I saw the man's left hand rise to his head and his glance move upward toward where the guard should have been. From behind him, I let out a small menacing growl, and as the man turned to face me, I jumped straight for his throat, sinking my deadly teeth into it to crush any possible sound of alarm he could have made. We hit the ground with me on top.

I released my hold on the dead man's destroyed, bloody throat and looked toward the direction of that menacing open bunkhouse door, waiting to see if anyone was going to answer the noise of the dead man and me hitting the ground …

No one appeared.

I jumped off the dead body and grabbed its leg just above the boot. Using my powerful jaws, I pulled the heavy load back into the dark shadows of the building. Not having a watch, and not being able to gain any idea of the time from the moon because of the mountainous walls on all sides, I had no idea of the time, but I was willing to bet that my last kill was the camp cook and that before long others would be waking. I suspected before too long, a couple of men would be heading out of the bunkhouse and over to the mess hall for a fast breakfast before relieving the night guards. One or both officers would soon be up and at it to make sure of the changing of the guards, to see to the breakfasting of the rest of the troops, and to begin organizing the daily duties. Before long, the fat was going to hit the fan. I was not going to be able to continue killing off the enemy one or two at a time.

I had successfully rescued Mrs. Custer from her captors, but the job was not finished yet. Now, somehow, single-handedly I had to keep her captors from going after her and bringing her back.

While keeping the bunkhouse watch, I figured it was time for a recount. My original recon spotted at least an even dozen. Tonight, at no time did I ever see any sign there were more than a dozen men, including the two officers. So far, I had removed the two gate guards, Mrs. Custer's guard, and two more soldiers for a total of five, leaving seven still alive.

I was still debating my next move when fate decided for me. I heard movement from the bunkhouse. As I watched, a form emerged from the darkened doorway; the form was in an officer's uniform.

Just as I recognized him as the junior officer, I watched him stop and take a general look around, and then he took a deliberate look upward at the guard posts and froze in disbelief as he discovered the absence of both guards.

I saw no way of taking him out covertly, so while watching him, for the sake of expediency, I turned from my present wolf form to my newly discovered wolf-man form and grabbed the Spencer. As I watched him turn back toward the bunkhouse doorway, most likely to raise the alarm, I did it for him by putting two very loud shots right into his back.

Before he could have said a word, two bloody roses sprung from his back as he was shoved very rudely into the dark opening of the bunkhouse door, with the exception of his boots, which I just barely had time to notice sliding into the bunkhouse. The window next to the doorway smashed out, and lead started flying all around in my direction.

Coolly, I took notice of the repeating flash of a face behind the flaming pistol in use. I took careful aim at the last place I had seen the face and fired back. The shooting stopped.

I barely had time to enjoy my accuracy when the shooting resumed. This shooter was being smart and shooting from deeper within the bunkhouse so I couldn't get a bead on him. Fortunately, this made his aim even worse than the first's. Unfortunately, while the bunkhouse didn't have a back door, it had windows all around. I could hear their plan in action. The shooter would keep me pinned down while others escaped the bunkhouse by busting out the windows, and then they would flank me.

Stepping back, I dropped the Spencer and changed from my wolf-man form into my golden eagle form and, with a mighty flap of my wings, I shot upward to land back at my perch overlook.

Sure enough, as the sun finally started reaching into the fortifications, I saw men charging from the side of the bunkhouse, guns-a-blazing, with more men appearing from the distant side the bunkhouse charging toward my last firing point, emboldened by a lack of return fire.

The men overran my last position and yelled an all clear. I observed the commanding officer walking out of the bunkhouse, pistol in hand.

The men could be seen literally scratching their heads over finding an empty set of duds and a spent Spencer lying on the ground. The commander came over, had a look, and began giving orders. From my perch, I could not hear the orders given, but I observed two men heading up toward the guard posts, and two men going into the center building. After a look around, the commander headed toward the center building as well. Before he got to the porch, the two men rushed out and anxiously reported their findings. I'm sure the commander had just been informed of the absence of Mrs. Custer.

Looking in the general direction of the open fort gates, the commander, appearing agitated, was giving more orders. The two men rushed off toward the back of the fort and out of sight.

I observed one of the two men that had rushed toward the guard post, now rushing back to the commander. Then, a blast knocked everyone to the ground and almost shook me from my perch. One or both men that had rushed off to the backside of the fort must have inspected the ammo building. I had rigged it to blow by just opening the door. Worried for the horses, I judged them far enough away from the ammo building to receive only a good scare.

While everyone was shatter-brained by my little surprise, I took flight. While the new guard was visibly trying to get to his feet, all alone, I charged him from above and hit him in the face like a large, winged bullet, knocking him over the fortifications to join the death ground of the earlier guards. Pushing the guard over the wall also allowed me to push off back into the wild blue yonder, out of both sight and shot of the only two survivors left.

I flew back to my perch in time to observe the man, who had been in the act of reporting to his commander, get up from the ground where the blast had planted him. He yelled something unheard as he went rushing by toward the corral of horses. This was one man with no fight left in him. It occurred to me that he might regain his fight and be a future problem.

I watched him rush around the center building, heading straight for the horses, and once he was behind the building and out of sight of the commander still standing on the center building's porch, I swooped down on him. As I was closing in for my attack, I let out a screech that turned him in my direction. He made a move for his side-iron, but what he saw froze him.

I was just feet above him and my momentum was shooting me right at him, I changed in mid-air into my wolf form and hit him so hard we both went rolling. My eagle claws had morphed into my wolf paws with their own set of claws of death, which I dug into his shoulders so deeply that even our inertia was not going to separate us.

Before he could even think of screaming, I had my jaws crushing his throat to a bloody mass of useless flesh, flesh I ripped out with relish, flesh a part of me was tempted to consume. I might have, except my humanity reminded me there was still one survivor with whom I must contend. Being the man in command, he might even be the smartest of my adversaries so far. I spat out the bloody heap of flesh that a part of me had enjoyed.

I jumped off the dead heap, and with my momentum carrying me upward, I changed back into my golden eagle form and flew up to my favored observation perch, only to discover that the commander was not to be seen.

Commander, oh commander, where art thou, commander?

From my perch, I moved.

Then I heard it. I looked in the direction of the open gate just in time to see a lone rider rushing through the open maw of the gateway. The commander must have found the saddled horse I had abandoned after I saw Mrs. Custer off. I bet he was riding right for Mrs. Custer, if only for revenge.

I took to the air, leaving the impenetrable fortress and all its death behind.

Chapter Fifteen
~ In Pursuit of Mrs. Custer ~

Once I cleared the mountain walls, I climbed even higher into the wild blue yonder and found my prey. He was going hell-bent-for-leather, pushing his mount for all he could. From my vantage point, high up and behind, he was riding so bent over the horse that his head and the horse's almost looked like one.

To catch him wasn't going to be easy, even with my mighty eagle wings. To gain ground on him, I swooped down from my high altitude and cut the distance between my prey and I in half. That wasn't going to be enough to catch up with him. Given time, I would not be able to maintain this speed. My survival sense told me I would use up my eagle fat trying. I swooped down to almost ground level and changed into my mighty wolf form.

In my wolf form, it appeared I could keep pace with horse and rider, but not gain. So for now, I was content just to follow my prey. At some point, horse and rider were going to have to take a break. I was betting in my wolf form he would have to take a break before I would, and when he did, then I would have him.

As the race went on, the sun rose higher and got hotter, and the race continued. As far as I could see, he had not looked back once. I didn't think he knew he was being trailed. He must have been crazed over losing Mrs. Custer and hell-bent on getting her back.

It seemed to me we were getting close to where Dawn had camped. Now, if she followed the plan when Mrs. Custer appeared, the two were to head straight north for Fort Wallace. This was dangerous territory, especially for two women alone. I figured Fort Wallace was closer, and from there the soldiers could take responsibility and see to returning Mrs.

92

Custer back to her husband.

Sure enough, the commander was slowing his mount. I slowed as I watched him dismount. I figured I'd slip in close and then...

War whoops.

I came to an abrupt stop and shot my glance to the left to see a party of six Indians charging down on the commander. I stopped, waited, and observed.

The commander, hearing them, stopped his investigation of Dawn's abandoned campsite. He jumped back into the saddle and the race was on again. This time, it was the Indians against the commander.

I trailed from a safe, unobserved position.

The commander apparently had removed his pistol and was firing backwards as his mount raced ahead. Indians whooped and charged after their prey, and I just kept trailing at quick clip. As I followed, I considered breaking off and heading north after the women, but the commander was in a world of trouble and leaving him to the merciless Indians did not seem right. Although what I, a lone werewolf, was going to do about six Indians was another thing.

The race continued.

Then the commander's horse stumbled and rolled, rider and horse together. I could see the horse was trying to get up as the commander, tossed a few feet ahead of his injured mount, rushed back to the horse and, forcing it back down, laid down to use the horse as cover and started firing his pistol.

Either because the Indians saw the end of their chase or because of the pistol firing, the Indians slowed their mounts. As they did, one Indian was shot off his horse and didn't get up. The Indians, still slowing, started firing back with rifles and bows and arrows. I could see arrows planting themselves into and near the prostrate, cantankerous horse. It was either not happy with the arrows penetrating its hide, the exploding shots behind its head, or both.

I then saw the commander toss his spent pistol out between the Indians and himself. He rose from behind the dead horse, hands raised in surrender. What was he thinking? He couldn't possibly think what was coming was going to go well for him.

As the Indians moved in, I kept my distance, watching. No one seemed to know I was near.

As the Indians dismounted their horses and gloated over their catch,

I moved to higher ground to watch what was coming next. Watch and, if possible, plan to rescue the commander, if only with a merciful death the Indians weren't going to give him.

While a couple of Indians tied the horses, the other three started undressing the commander. They tossed and inspected each bit of clothes stripped from their prey. When they finished inspecting his Confederate hat, coat, and shirt, they threw him to the ground and started in on his boots and pants, laughing the whole time over their spoils and possibly jabbering in anticipation over what was coming next.

The commander stayed stoic through the whole rape and humiliation. Having an idea of what was coming next, I couldn't help but wonder how long that would last.

The Indians then went about tying down the commander with arms and legs outstretched. Remembering that one messenger I had found being tortured by Indians, I did not want to stick around to witness what was coming next, but I felt it my human duty to try to come to the aid of a fellow human being, if only to grant him a quicker death than the Indians were going to grant him.

I noticed the Indians had left their bows and arrows with the horses. I also noticed they had not left their rifles with the horses, with the exception of the rifle in the hands of the horse guard. Maybe I could slip down and steal a set, and from a distance plant some arrows in the commander. The problem with that plan was the Indian staying with the horses. Once I revealed myself, what chance would I have against this mini war party?

I kept watching and biding my time.

Once the Indians had their captive properly tied down, they ate lunch. I couldn't believe my eyes. The Indians sat around, feasting on beef strips and hard bread, while continuing their jovialities over their plans for a torturous, fun-filled dessert.

After satisfying their thirsts riverside, it was time for the show to begin: as three Indians looked on, the one that must have been their leader pulled out his large-bladed knife and set to removing the commander's scalp. To the commander's credit, he didn't let out a scream. Too bad for the commander. From what I have learned, Indians like to see just how long a brave man will last under torture. The braver the victim, the longer the torture is prolonged in honor of the brave one being tortured. I had heard some horrifying stories around the campfire shared with Union trackers during my war years. Now I was about to witness it for myself, if I couldn't come up with some merciful intervention for the commander.

Once the scalp was removed, the Indian leader showed it off proudly to the others, then looped the hair around his rawhide belt and started slowly, with feeling, carving the commander's chest. Still, no screams came from the commander. Either he was a very brave man or just very bullheaded against giving his captors any satisfaction. Even from my distance, my animal olfactory nerves could smell the fear coming off him in waves. From my vantage point, I didn't see much blood coming from the chest cuts, which had me thinking the cuts were most likely shallow, and the torturer was still just playing with his victim. The real fun hadn't even begun yet.

The lead torturer and his audience walked over to the river and helped themselves to another drink, notably taking their time at it, giving the tortured more time to consider what was to come. They calmly walked back to the commander, the torturer making a point of again removing his large knife, only then returning to his kneeling position beside the one to be tortured.

Not wanting his victim to miss anything, the torturer lifted the right eyelid and, with a quick, decisive movement, sliced it off. The commander's head jerked, but he still refused to scream. The torturer performed the same operation on other eyelid. It occurred to me that if these proceedings lasted very long, the commander would most likely die a blind man, as a result of the bright sun and no eyelids behind which to hide. Why? Did the torturer want to expose the victim to the sun or to make him watch the torture?

The torture continued.

Tossing the eyelids away, the torturer suddenly slammed down the knife blade right into the commander's left upper arm, and, as screaming commenced, the torturer pulled the knife from a little below the shoulder down to the elbow. It looked like the torturer was playing the knife around the sliced open arm and the commander screamed more.

The torturer, with a flourish, moved the knife to his other hand to jam the blade into the commander's left upper leg and the commander screamed more.

At this point, his audience had moved in and obstructed my view, thank God.

I noticed the Indian assigned to watch the horses had become engrossed in the proceedings and had moved a few feet, to try to gain a better view of the proceedings. Possibly, this could be to my advantage.

As the torture continued and the commander continued screaming out his lungs, I changed to human form and eased down behind the horses. I figured I could only do this in human form and not scare the horses. Any of my animal forms would have frightened them.

As I came up to the horses, I touched them friendly-like, and they simply moved a bit to give me room and to allow me to move past them. Some feet ahead of me was the guard so totally enthralled with the proceedings that he failed to hear the gentle movement of the horses. The commander's screaming was a help. It both helped hide sounds of my movement, and kept the Indian who was supposed to be watching the horses too enthralled with what was happening in front of him to see what was about to happen to him from behind.

As I came up to the Indian's exposed back, I changed into wolf-man form and used my clawed hand to rip out his throat. As he slowly sank to the ground, making a gurgling sound not likely to be heard over the commander's screaming, I reached for the rifle in the dead hand. Noticing one of the audience was calmly turning my way, I shot him. The 44. cal hit him in the chest with such a punch the Indian fell backwards, over the torturer and his victim.

The rifle was a front loader and only good for one shot. I turned the rifle around and charged into the last two standing Indians. My wolf-man appearance gave me the upper hand. As they had turned, one reached for his knife and the other raised his rifle, but both froze at the sight of the monstrous, half-man, half-wolf aberration charging them.

Taking full advantage of their joint immobilization, I clubbed the rifle owner so hard that parts of his head and brains went in a different direction than the rest of the corpse. I turned just in time to bring up the rifle, still in my hand, and in a two-handed fashion, I blocked the downward motion of the knife originally aiming for my back.

I shoved my hands upward with such force that the knife went flying. The Indian tried to counter by grabbing for the rifle, separating us, so I let him have it. Before he could register what had happened, I grabbed the Indian's head with both wolf claws and squeezed with such force his eyes literally popped out. Blood gushed from his eye holes, nose, and ears. When his life popped free of this newly formed corpse, I let it drop to the ground.

All that was left was the torturous leader. I noticed him roll away and come to his feet, his large bloody knife in hand, with blood from the commander dripping from point to hilt. I pledged this one wasn't going to die easily and changed into my grizzly bear form. I figured seeing me change right in front of him would scare the hell out of him just before I sent him there.

Not taken aback by my morphing in front of him, the Indian suddenly charged me with his knife raised for a downward strike. I simply reached outward, grabbed hold of the wrist with the large, blooded knife, and squeezed until I heard his wrist bones crushing. With a little twist, the Indian's prized torture device went flying as a bone popped out of his crushed wrist.

While I still had his crushed wrist in my hand, he swung a blow at my face with his other fisted hand. I caught it in my wide-open mouth and bit down so hard on it that I totally separated his fist from the rest of his body. I spit it out in his screaming face.

His reaction was a disappointment. He passed out. After all the scary tales I had heard about how tough Indians were, this one ruined my fun by passing out. The sudden quiet was broken by the slight sound of moaning coming from my feet. Looking down, I discovered the moaning came from the commander. He was alive, if only barely. I discovered what I had been missing when the audience moved in for a better view of the torture. His legs had gotten the same treatment as his arm. Both legs were sliced open, from groin to knees. With all that blood loss, I had to wonder how it was he still lived, like the Indian.

I looked back to the Indian and realized just how much blood he was losing from both wrists, especially the one limply at his side, the one missing a hand.

I slapped the Indian across the face and received something of a weak reaction. My fun with him was over. I curved my hand, palm up, claws out, and knifed my hand into the Indian's upper stomach, just below his ribs. This got a reaction from him. His eyes smacked open in surprise, which only matched his screams as my claws reached in and upward until I found a part of him beating in my hand.

With one quick movement, I pulled his beating heart out of his lower chest and showed it to his shocked face. As he died, I tossed both the Indian corpse and his dead heart away in disgust. For such a great and mighty torturer of others, he had not lasted long on the receiving end.

Changing back to human form, I knelt down to inspect the commander, but there really wasn't anything to be done for the man.

His eyes were open; they looked at me and glazed over. He was gone. I recalled the army trackers would say, "He's made wolf's meat.' Now I understood that saying because I had nothing to bury him with, I'd have to leave him and the Indian carcasses to feed the wolves or any other carnivorous beasties.

It occurred to me I was one bloody mess, so I walked over to the river, jumped in, and feverishly went about rubbing all that blood off me. After my wash, I got myself a good, deep drink and let the sun dry me.

The next thing I had to do was get me some clothes. I didn't like the idea much, but the only civilized clothes was the Confederate uniform the Indians had removed from the commander, but had not taken the time to parcel out. I was pleasantly surprised at the discovery of the Spencer rifle the one Indian was about to use on me, but hadn't been given the chance. The Spencer wasn't as good a rifle as my Henry repeater, but it was much better than the muzzleloader the horse guard had been toting. The Indian also had a pouch on his rawhide belt that contained enough rounds for a couple of Spencer reloads. Considering the Indian most likely stole the weapon and ammo off a dead soldier, one he probably killed himself, and seeing I was retired military, I had no qualms about taking the ill-gotten lot for myself.

As for transportation, I had plenty of horses from whom to choose. Not crazy about traveling Indian-style, I walked over to the commander's dead steed and unfastened the saddle from the dead horse. That was the easy part. Part of the saddle was under the dead mass of horseflesh. There was nothing I could do but grab hold of the saddle and pull with all my might and hope it came free. It came free with such ease I almost fell backward with saddle in hand. I guess I still needed to learn my own strength.

Saddle in hand, I walked over to the Indian horses and picked out the two that look the strongest and the fastest: I still wanted to catch up with Mrs. Custer and Dawn as fast as possible, which might mean running a horse as long as possible, then switching to the second one for a fresher mount. Once the horse was saddled, I looked toward the dead.

I had no time to bury them and nothing to use to dig a grave. Hell, there weren't even enough rocks around to bury even one, so I gathered the horse blankets off the spare horses, and, after freeing them, I took their blankets and placed them over the dead. With regret, I left them as wolf meat.

With due consideration to the heat and sun, I walked over and gathered up the commander's Confederate hat and walked back to the horses. Saddling up, I tipped my hat to the dead and gave chase northward toward the women. What had happened to the commander only served to increase my concern over the two women traveling alone in this dangerous territory. Heading north, I charged off, riding hard.

Come nightfall I still had not sighted two women and a wagon, but as I was considering camping for the night to rest the horses and possibly hunt for something to eat, in wolf form perhaps, I spotted the distant glow of a campfire. Could it be the women? Then I remembered that Dawn, like most, if not all, prairie Indians, knew to dig a small ditch in which to build a campfire so the fire's flames were not visible for miles around because of the flatness of the prairie. Most likely, this was not an Indian encampment either.

Approaching slowly, I considered leaving the horses and going to recon in coyote or eagle form, but I was worried I might lose them, so I decided not to leave them. I approached the campfire slowly, carefully, and with the rifle cocked and ready to fire just in case.

As I neared the campfire, by its glow I was able to make out the form of men in dark clothes, blue belles, soldiers. Most likely, from the fact there were only two and the camp lacked military order, these were deserters. By now, they had already seen me.

"Ahoy in the camp. I'm alone and just looking for some rest and good conversation," I called ahead.

"Well, come on in."

I dismounted and walked in, my hand still near the trigger of the Spencer.

I had not considered the Confederate uniform.

"He's a reb!" They both went for their side arms. I ducked to make myself less of a target and shot the first one in the chest.

The second one was smart enough to dodge away from the fire and into the cover of the darkness of the night. The first time he fired at me, I fired back where I had seen the flash of his pistol and must have nailed him good, judging by the sound of his scream.

"Stop shooting, Reb. I'm dead. You gut-shot me good."

I carefully walked in the direction of the flash. As I neared the fire, I could see the other. His face was gone. I got to figuring that I aimed for his chest, and he must have ducked face-first into my return fire.

Nearing the second, I shuffled a bit sideways, placing myself near the fire, where I removed a burning stick for the light. Then I moved toward the sound of groaning.

As I neared, the soldier groaned. "You got me good, Reb!" He coughed.

I waved the burning stick near him. Having a close look at his injury, I saw his stomach was a mess. He was trying to hold his guts in, but I could see both guts and blood leaking between his fingers. A 56-56 round at such close range did a powerful load of damage on a personage. I had seen enough such injuries during the war. Even if there was a surgeon around, he didn't stand a chance.

"To begin with, I'm not a Confederate. I took this from a man who was being tortured by Indians. He had no use for it."

He tried to laugh, but only blood came out.

Despite his condition, I wanted information. "Seen two women: one white, one Indian, traveling with a wagon?"

He croaked out a bloody, "Yes ... gave them ... direc ... for ... Fo ...Walla ..." He died.

So, at least I knew the women had been doing well earlier in the day and given directions for Fort Wallace.

I saw to the horses, only to discover that they had bolted during the firefight and by now were most likely well gone. Searching the encampment, I easily discovered where the men had corralled their horses. At least I had fresh mounts come sunrise. I also soon discovered one of the men knew how to make good coffee.

After enjoying a couple of cups of the fine coffee, I tossed some water from a canteen on the fire, killing it so no one else would spot the improperly prepared fire as I had. Then I set about getting some sleep.

Come sunrise I checked on the condition of the uniform the corpse with no face was wearing. It occurred to me that a change in uniform might be warranted, especially after last night's fireworks just because of my borrowed duds. The uniform was a bit worse than the grey uniform I was wearing, but appeared to be free of bugs or lice at least. I undressed the dead soldier and redressed in the more popular uniform of the Union blue. I also took on the proper Union belt and side arm the faceless one provided. His hat was a bloody mess, but I found the hat belonging to the other soldier and made use of it. Then I saw to the horses.

The horses seemed well rested, fed and ready to go, so I saddled both horses so I wouldn't have to bother later unsaddling one to re-saddle the second when switching. All preparations done, I pointed the horses northward and charged off with the goal of either catching up with the women or arriving at Fort Wallace soon after them.

The day's travel was long, hot, and uneventful. Not having anything with me to eat, and only one canteen of water, I didn't bother with a nooner. I kept traveling. I did make a point of changing horses from time to time, so as not to overtire either horse.

The following nightfall, just as I was considering calling it a day, I spied in the distance what could be a wagon being trailed by two horses, possibly Horse and Mrs. Custer's horse. I sped up my pace and, as the sun was calling it a day, I saw the wagon with two trailing horses ahead. I could even make out two forms in the wagon. I was tempted to fire off a couple of shots to announce my presence, but most likely, I'd scare the women and possibly announce my presence to some distant company not wanted. So, I figured I'd continue on and eventually catch up with them after they camped for the night.

My horse was getting real lathered up and showing signs of wearing out, so I stopped and changed horses again. Even with night coming on, I figured if I continued, I'd come upon their camp in the dark.

Some hours later, I slowed my horse's pace, as I smelled smoke and suspected I was nearing my goal. Then, an arrow twanged right past my ear.

"Who there? Arrow hit chest," a familiar female voice announced from the darkness ahead.

"Is that any way to greet a Skin-walker?" I happily called back. The word 'Skin-walker' was out before I remembered Mrs. Custer and her possibly overhearing me.

"Captain Cody. No recognize. Come," a jovial, voice called back.

I happily did Dawn's bidding, and, while I was dismounting, Dawn joined my side with bow still in hand and a quiver of arrows strapped to her back.

"I happy see you."

I looked at the bow and quiver of arrows. "Been having problems?"

"Trouble with two blue coats. We safe."

I remembered a black eye on the soldier shot in the gut that the firefight had not put there. "They gave me some difficulties too…They're past worrying about it now." Having noticed the *we*, I wondered. "You're looking in good shape. How's Mrs. Custer? For that matter, where is Mrs. Custer?"

"She fine. She sleep wagon, too good for sleep ground."

"Tell me of this difficulty with soldiers?"

"No."

My stomach interrupted our catching up. "Any grub? I haven't eaten in days. Been too busy trying to catch up with you two ladies to take time to hunt."

Right now, even Dawn's veggie stew was going to taste good. I just had to remember to enjoy it, but not ask what was in it.

She marched me over to the campfire and slapped something into a wooden bowl, and I got to thinking I would probably better enjoy her stew since I couldn't see what I was eating.

As I ate, Dawn just sat and let me eat in peace. Afterward, I changed into my own clothes and my own boots, hat, and pistol belt. I finally felt like my old self once I had that good old feeling of my own side arm at my hip.

I took the two horses I had come with and started to unsaddle them, but a big old friendly muzzle of my old friend and sidekick rudely interrupted me. "Horse!"

After happily giving him the attention he needed, I went back to unsaddling the two very tired horses. I almost didn't bother to hobble the two, as they were so obviously too tired to wander far.

When I got back to the campfire, Dawn had already gotten out my bedroll and laid it out near the fire. Then she had planted herself down against a wagon wheel, with bow across her lap and quiver of arrows at her side in easy reach. She was sitting guard duty as Mrs. Custer and I slept. I figured if she felt the need, she'd wake me and get herself some sleep. The rest of the night was uneventful. Dawn let me sleep through the night uninterrupted.

Come the rising of the sun, we set off for Fort Wallace. Mrs. Custer and Dawn rode in the wagon, and I rode point on Horse where I belonged, out front of the wagon. The other horses followed, tied to the back of the wagon. Having the horses in tow worried me a little if we had to make a run from Indians, but horseflesh was still at a premium in the area because of the war.

Two days of uneventful traveling found us within sight of Fort Wallace. All this time and the fort did not look much improved. The portal to the parade grounds looked slimmer, but there were still no gates to the fortifications. There was one other notable change.

Just like the other fort, outside of this one was a sizable Indian encampment. The first time, I didn't think much about it, but seeing an Indian encampment outside not one but two forts was just too strange to ignore, especially during these times of Indian uprisings.

My first concern was to get Mrs. Custer to the care and responsibility of the soldiers and, frankly, I was looking forward to a number of tall drinks at the fort's outpost. I heeled Horse and started for the fort, and came to a total halt at Dawn's calling hoots. The wagon with the women hadn't moved an inch. Then I remembered. Dawn was not welcomed within Fort Wallace.

I walked Horse back toward the wagon and talked directly to Mrs. Custer. "Ma'am, I'd be mighty pleased if you'd saddle up on one of the extra horses and take yourself into the fort's protection."

"But sir, surely the acting camp commander will want to thank you for freeing me from that army of ruffians!" Mrs. Custer exclaimed.

"Most likely so, ma'am, but they would not take to kindly to Dawn's presence. I'd just as rather you rode in alone and allowed Dawn and me to be on our way, no fuss."

"If that is the way you want it, who am I to argue with the man who probably saved my life." Looking at Dawn, she added, "And the woman who saved me from those two deserter scum."

Dawn just looked back, saying nothing.

I turned Mrs. Custer's attention back to me. "Mrs. Custer, if you would not mind, could you take these extra horses to rein? It would be my pleasure if you'd explain how I came by these horses the deserters stole."

"Why, that would be my pleasure, sir."

Twenty minutes later, as Dawn and I watched, Mrs. Custer rode up to the posted guards. Without taking my glance off Mrs. Custer and while also noticing another soldier walking the other horses back to the camp corral, I turned to Dawn.

"Seems strange seeing all those Indians encamped next to all these forts. First Fort Riley and now Fort Wallace. Any ideas why?"

"Jumlin's children."

Chapter Sixteen
~ Jumlin's Children ~

"Who or what are Jumlin's children?"

"See tepee with signs?" Dawn answered.

"Chief's tepee?"

"No, Shaman. Medicine man. We visit, answer all questions."

"Won't he notice I'm different?" I remembered her warnings about Indians not liking my presence, not to mention that incident with the gambling house girl.

"Yes, he know me. He know you good spirit."

It occurred to me that what she wasn't saying was this medicine man knew her grandfather. Indians don't speak of their dead, so I didn't ask.

I allowed her to lead us into the Indian encampment and to lead me into the shaman's tepee. Once inside, she sat quietly to the side to let us men of magic speak.

Before I could speak, he spoke in English. "I know you Skin-walker. I feel strong good spirit. You bring bad medicine those around you. You bring Jumlin's children here."

He gave me a moment to take in his words. "Jumlin's children sense your mighty magic. Jumlin's children come challenge your magic. Jumlin's children come challenge you."

"Please, tell me who are these Jumlin's children?"

"Blood feeder of warriors. Rapist of women. Stealer of children. Offspring of demon." After letting me digest that, he continued. "Legends say medicine man love became one with woman. They live, love, led people well. In time, it clear medicine man's woman barren. She bring forth no child. Medicine man plead Great Spirit for child. Medicine man's woman still barren.

105

"As medicine man's woman grow old, medicine man challenge Great Spirit for child. His woman still barren.

"Medicine man, feel forsaken by Great Spirit. Abandon Great Spirit and meditate with evil spirits. Evil spirit promise medicine man children. He demand own medicine man spirit for short time. The medicine man desperate. Did as evil spirit say and make forbidden rituals. Brought evil spirit here. Allow evil spirit to take medicine man. Evil spirit lie to medicine man. He take medicine man's body.

"Evil spirit name Jumlin. Jumlin make children with woman. Jumlin feed on blood of warriors and women to live. Jumlin's children feed on blood of warriors and women like father to live long life.

"Jumlin and children rape and steal children of raped women for Jumlin's blood stealers tribe. Warriors and raped women die, tribe die. Jumlin and Jumlin's children move next tribe. Feed and grow. Jumlin's tribe rape and steal children.

"Legend say mighty tribe of warriors kill Jumlin before Jumlin's children kill off tribe. Jumlin's children take mighty tribe's women. Women die, Jumlin's children move."

Finding this tale hard to throw a lasso around, I interrupted. "Legends are just stories—"

"No! Jumlin's children not stories. Jumlin's children not heard for many, many moons. Jumlin's children return. Indian nation of many tribes. Many tribes no more.

"Warriors fight blue coats over sacred lands, now hunt Jumlin's children. Jumlin's children sense strong magic warrior spirit. Your warrior magic spirit challenge their evil spirits. Jumlin's children come for you."

"How do you know Jumlin's children are here?"

"Find whole tribes dried like corn husks let dry. Tribes with no blood found."

"You say this has not happened for many years? So, where have these Jumlin's children been all this time?"

"Jumlin's children hide in great mountain. Great Spirit's sun power burn Jumlin's children like stick in fire. Children of evil one do evil in night."

Inside the mountains not far from Denver. That fit with the talk in the gambling house of leaving the mountain area alone because of numbers of men who never came out of those hills.

"So, if they can't do their evil in the light of day, how do they survive away from their mountain out in the great wide open prairies?"

"They burrow in ground like prairie dogs before Great Sun wake for day. They come out ground, do evil after Great Spirit's eye sleeps. Dried tribes found in bed. Die in sleep."

I recalled the stories in the gambling house of a mountain area now considered taboo for all gold diggers. "If Jumlin's children have been hiding out in the mountains for years, how have they fed themselves?"

"Not know. They here. Sense great warrior spirit. If good spirit disturbs them it possible they feed off evil waves from white man war and Indian wars with white man."

I was still having a little problem with the idea of blood-feeding, half-demonic children, but if I could exist as a Skin-walker, then demonic children could be possible. "Okay, if sunlight kills, then I suspect so does fire. Any other ways to kill these bloodsuckers? How was Jumlin killed?"

"Jumlin legends say, speared through heart. No die until beheaded. Know not children. Children of demon maybe like demonic father in killing. This maybe for Skin-walker to learn."

Doubt may have showed on my face. "See for self. Leave here, go four moons to setting sun. Travel with sun on left side of horse. Find village of dried out husks. Beware, you in sacred hunting grounds. You not welcome."

As I was about to get up to leave, the old man spoke again. "Wait, I have thing may help you."

I sat back down as the old medicine man pulled out two necklaces from behind him. "This may protect you from Jumlin's children." The two necklaces were just alike, and I had the feeling they may have been made recently. I examined them.

"Shields bear symbols of sun and symbol to ward off evil."

The circular necklaces had a symbol that look like a sun, and, within the sun symbol was another symbol that looked like two arrows facing each other with a dot between them.

"Wear them well," the medicine man said in a grave voice. "They keep you live."

Chapter Seventeen
~ Village of Husks ~

Following the shaman's directions, after four days of traveling west and about a day and a half traveling north, I spied the inverted "V" of tepees. The sun was almost at its highest point when we got near enough to see for sure that it was a village of tepees, and only a village of tepees. I saw no sign of life anywhere; there were none of the typical signs of village life. No children playing, no women going about their chores, nor was there any sign of horses.

Long before we reached the village, the stench of death reached us. Before we neared it, I had to raise my war rag from around my neck, place it over my nose and mouth, and start breathing through my mouth instead of my nose. I realized this must give me the look of a holdup man, but I really didn't figure on anyone alive in the village to see me. I looked back at Dawn. She took it like an Indian, with stoic indifference except for her eyes. I was concerned by the betrayal of her eyes.

I turned Horse around and doubled back to the wagon and Dawn. "Maybe you should stay here while I look around the village. You can keep a wary eye out for anyone unfriendly."

She just nodded in the affirmative. I almost suggested she move farther away from the village, some distance away from the stench of the place, but then she'd be too far away to watch my back. We'd been lucky so far. We hadn't run into any unfriendliness such as Indian war parties or Jumlin's children. I couldn't help but wonder when our luck was going to run out.

I walked Horse in slowly so I could take time to overlook the village and have time to react to any surprises that might pop up. The only surprise I got was from Horse, who came to a complete stop outside the village and refused to move any further. Horse and I had ridden over and through many a battlefield over the years, battlefields ripe with dead and wounded, some screaming for help and Horse had never once hesitated from his duties, like a true warhorse.

Horse made it very clear he was not going into this village under any circumstances. Not having any choice in the matter, I dismounted Horse, removed my Henry repeating rifle from its scabbard, and walked into the village alone.

At first sight, the village looked peaceful and quiet, not a sign that anything was wrong, until I saw her. Just outside of one of the tepees was the prone form of a woman. I rushed to her aid and noticed her ragged clothes, which had been torn from the front of her body. This woman had been brutally raped. As I got closer, it was clear she'd been killed as well. She was extremely pale. At first glance, I wondered who or what would rape and kill an old woman.

Deep wrinkles pitted her aged face. Reaching her side, I found she was not an old woman. She had the hair and clothes of a young woman of childbearing age. She had that aged appearance because her skin was totally dried out. I touched the skin and discovered it as dry as the great desert. Closer examination showed no obvious signs of trauma, until I got to her neck. There were two bite marks on the side of her neck as if a snake had bitten her. A very large snake because the two punctures were so wide apart. She had a look of pure panic on her dried up face. She had not died in her sleep.

Looking around, I found where some animal hide had been left out to dry after skinning. I rushed over, grabbed it up, and walked back to the raped corpse to cover her shame with the hide. While doing so, I accidentally brushed her skin. It was like touching the backside of the animal hide I was placing over her. The animal hide had not yet been properly cured to soften and make it fit for whatever use she had intended.

I chose the tepee from which she had been pulled to investigate first. Inside, I found a man and a baby. Both looked like they were still sleeping. I half expected the man to wake up and attack me for being an intruder inside his dwelling, but it didn't happen. On closer examination, I saw both father and child had the same dried out look as the woman outside. They both had bite marks like the woman, except that the baby's was on its once plump, little, dried-up leg.

I was on my fourth inspection of the tepees when it hit me. These dead should have made a smorgasbord for any carrion creatures like coyotes, foxes, wolves and a whole lot more. There was no sign any animal had been anywhere near this village. As much as this village of the dead smelled, it should have attracted carrion creatures from miles around. Even creepier was the realization that there weren't even any flies around. That did it. I gave in to the creeps and rushed out of the tepee to leave the village long enough to look for trails showing which way the renegades went after leaving this village of the dead.

Circling the village many times, I found that it became stranger and stranger. There were no tracks anywhere. No horse tracks, no moccasin tracks, not even any tracks from bare feet. Nothing.

I found the makeshift corral where the villagers kept their horses. One side of the corral had been busted out where the panicked horses had broken out of the corral and headed out for the safety of the great wide-open plains. From the look of the tracks, the horses, once free, scattered. I looked back from the corral to the village and wondered how the villagers had failed to hear the commotion the horses must have been making even before they panicked enough to bust out of the corral. Very strange

Since I hadn't checked all the tepees for clues, I reluctantly returned to my investigations and moseyed back to the two tepees not yet searched.

Within the first of the two, I found a body as pale as the rest of the goners, but it didn't have that dried out look. It didn't appear to be drained of blood like every other villager I had searched, from eldest to baby. I started to move the corpse closer to the light coming in through the tepee's center hole for a better look. Suddenly, the corpse attacked me.

Its eyes popped open and the hands of the living corpse flew up at an unnatural speed and locked my throat in a vise grip. I morphed into my wolf-man form, making my neck larger, stronger, and harder to crush. This fiend definitely was trying to crush my throat.

Remembering what the medicine man said about sunlight, I latched onto its arms and pulled the fiend toward the light coming into the tepee. As his arm reached near the light, the creature released its death grip and tried to move away from me, but now I was the dominant force. We continued our death tug-of-war. As the pale, naked arm of my assailant reached the light, the arm flamed like dry brush hit by lightning.

The creature bared his teeth and went for my throat, fangs leading the attack. I fell backward and sideways, leading the creature right into the light, where it flamed enough to singe the fur of my hands and wrist. I quickly tossed the burning corpse from me before my clothes began burning.

For now, I watched as the corpse burned to a fanged skeleton. Then even that burned until nothing remained but burnt ashes and an unpleasant memory of the attacker. I discovered the tepee had started to burn, so I made a quick exit out into the very comforting light of day.

There was yet one more tepee to search, but I'd had my fill of this village of husks and its hidden fiends from hell. I picked up a stick, let the burning tepee flame the stick, and touched it to the last of the tepees not inspected, the only one that wouldn't stand inspection. A scream that could only originate from a creature from hell came forth from the burning tepee.

Well, another one of Jumlin's children bites the dust. Or should I say, is turned to dust. I burned all the tepees, totally destroying this creation from hell, this village of husks.

With the village in flames, I stood back, inspected my handiwork, and made sure the entire village turned to dust and burnt ruins.

Considering the possibility that other creatures from hell might have heard the screams from the last tepee, I figured our best move was to make beaver out of the area before nightfall!

I figured we really needed to get the wiggle on, as nightfall was only a couple hours off, but I was just too dragged out to bother. I walked up to Horse, who, true to form for a warhorse, was just where I left him. I started to saddle up when I stopped and reached into my saddlebag. Pulling out the amulet the medicine man had given me that I had placed there for safekeeping, I put it on. Then I slumped into the saddle, turned Horse south, and let him follow his head toward a lake we had passed to get here. It seemed like days ago now.

I passed Dawn without sharing a word and hardly bothered to take notice of her turning the wagon rig my direction and following in silence. When we reached the lake, I dismounted Horse, got to unsaddling him, and set to preparing an encampment for the night. Dawn did the same. Neither of us bothered to speak to the other; I was too dragged out for conversation.

After the encampment was ready, Dawn grabbed a stick from the pile of future firewood and walked out to all four sides of the encampment, drawing a symbol like that on our necklaces into the ground. I guessed she figured no night fiend was going to sneak in and attack us in our sleep with those symbols engraved into the earth. I hoped she was right.

Chapter Eighteen
~ After Jumlin's Children ~

Dawn had the right idea with her engraved artwork in the dirt because we had an uneventful and restful night's sleep. I possibly got more rest than Dawn. She rested sitting up against a wagon wheel with bow and arrows easily at hand as I slept. Come the rising of the sun, I felt like a new man, a new man with a major problem: How do you find a tribe of blood-sucking demonic Indians that burrow into the ground by day? Answer—you let them come to you, but from inside an impenetrable fortress so you don't make it easy for them.

We decamped and headed southeast toward Kansas and an old battleground hideaway within a mountain.

After two days traveling, we found trouble. From my usual position a fair distance ahead of Dawn and the wagon, I saw it first. At first, I wasn't sure what it was. It could be a small battlefield. Possible bodies disrupted the flat open ground ahead, with spears protruding from the ground. As we got close enough for a better look, Horse came to a halt and refused to continue just like at the village of husks.

I took Horse back to the wagon. On approaching, I dismounted. "Dawn, it looks like there may have been a fight up ahead. Horse refused to go any farther, just like at the village. I'm going in to investigate."

With some reluctance, I went forth to discover what looked, the closer I got to it, like a fight between killkenny cats. A half-dozen Indians were all spread out, and more arrows than I could count spread out over the area. The battleground included some spears protruding from the ground, which was what had caught my attention at first. Normally, I wouldn't care a continental about a lot of dead Indians, but closer examination showed these Indians to be dried out.

Even more interesting was the Indian pinned to the ground by a spear. It was a skeleton with fangs. That's when I realized the fanged Indian had been speared through the heart. I guessed that the spear in the heart killed this Jumlin's child, and the body burned to bones with the rising of the sun, or he was just pinned and later killed with the rising of the sun. The sight reminded me of what the medicine man said about the death of Jumlin: "Legends say Jumlin speared through heart, but not die until beheaded." I gathered up the spears and walked back to the wagon.

"What you find?" Dawn said.

"A passel of dead dried up Indians. There's also an Indian skeleton with fangs and a spear through its heart—or where the heart used to be. I think it was a hunting party that got dry-gulched. I don't believe it was a war party. The dead Indians aren't wearing war paint."

"Dry-gulched?"

"Ambushed. It looks like the hunting party was ambushed. There are signs of disrupted soil, like someone or something came out of the ground and attacked those Indians."

"What we do now?"

"These spears look like good weapons against those bloodsuckers. I'm going to put them in the wagon, and then I'm going to retrieve the shovel from the wagon and bury the dead." I started for the back of the wagon when I stopped. "You can watch my back from here." Then I went to put the spears in the back of the wagon and ferret out the shovel.

I didn't look forward to returning to Dry Gulch, but I felt the dead needed to be buried. So I went about digging a large hole, and once finished, I got to the unpleasant task of carrying or dragging the dried out Indians to the burial pit.

Once completed, I really had an unpleasant task—touching the fanged Indian skeleton so I could drag it to the pit. Once done, I started to remove the spear from the fanged one's chest. Somehow, it seemed a better idea to leave the thing speared. I broke off the spear and rolled the foul creature into the burial pit. I had a pang of regret over planting that foul thing with the humans, but I had no time for two burial sites because the sun was starting to set over the mountains to the west of us. I was just about finished filling in the burial site, when I heard a groan from something that could only have come from hell.

I turned to see, not one, but two fanged Indians lunging for me. As they neared, my amulet actually glowed and the two fiends froze. The closest one put his arms over his face to ward off the glowing amulet.

More out of reflex than thought, I grabbed up the broken end of the spear at my feet and plunged it deep into the fiend's chest just as something flung past me and plunged into the eye of the second fiend. It screamed, but didn't go down like the one I had just speared.

I quickly removed my Union sword from its scabbard and, as the fiend with the arrow stood in front of me, I moved forward, nearing my target and in one strong, wide arc, I sliced the fiend's head from its shoulders. As the beast went down and its head rolled away, I was again reminded of what the medicine man had said. "Legends say Jumlin speared through heart, but not die until beheaded."

So, I beheaded the other of the two attacking fiends and stepped back from my ugly task. Dawn was suddenly at my side as I was contemplating whether beheading was important enough to dig up the fiend already buried or not.

"Nice shooting, hitting that thing in the eye like that."

"I aim for chest," she said.

"Well, it gave me the time to finish the job before he finished me. Did you see this amulet glow at their presence?"

"No. I see them stop before you. Where they come from?"

"The ground. Once the sun passed over the mountains, they came out from under the ground." Then I got thinking about the two incidents, here and at the village of dried up Indians. In both cases, a couple of bloodsuckers were left behind. Then it occurred to me. They were over-bloated from feeding.

As a kid, I had removed ticks from a friend's dog, and I had noticed the ticks full of blood acted dragged out, because they were overly filled with blood. In both cases where I had come across the victims of Jumlin's children, a couple of the fiends had been left behind. I'd bet they were ones that had overfed and, bloated with fresh blood, had burrowed in the ground to sleep off their overfeeding instead of going on with the main group.

Worse, it had just occurred to me that they were not somewhere behind us, but somewhere in front of us. Could they be setting up a Dry Gulch for us?

"Dawn, set up a dry camp, no fire. Do your drawing in the dirt thing, and keep your eyes open and alert. I'm going to do an eagle recon of the area."

Instructions given, I deliberately forgot about the two fiends needing burial and the idea of digging up the other to behead it. I jumped into the back of the wagon and shed clothes while morphing into the Golden Eagle. As expected, the amulet continued to hang around my neck.

In eagle form, I jumped up onto the wagon bench and, with a mighty flap of my wings, was off soaring into the dark night. The first thing I did was to perform recon circles around Dawn's encampment in ever-growing loops, looking for any activity in the immediate area. There was none to be seen, including a noticeable lack of wildlife. It was as if even the wild animals knew to avoid the area of this evil.

I spotted some fish in the stream nearby, and since the area seemed clear of danger, I took the time for a fish dinner, which was so good; I had a second fish dinner and a drink of water. Then I went back on the hunt.

Look for trouble and you'll find trouble. In the distance, I spotted fires, most likely campfires. Maybe an Indian encampment. I decided to have a look.

I flew toward the fires and over a total shindy within an Indian village. At first sight, it looked like a war between Indians. It was difficult to see who was who, so I perched on one of the tepees. The first Indian I saw bared fangs, and I figured it was time to put a spike in the wheel by entering a little supernatural ingredient into this battle. I swooped down, changed into my grizzly bear form, and marched out from the dark of the tepee.

I grabbed the fanged fiend, turned it around, and ripped into its chest to remove its dark imitation of a heart. I tossed it away and grabbed the fiend's head and ripped it off. With blood spurting in multiple directions, the fiend dropped dead, and the human Indian victim I saved was gone. Can you imagine him trying to tell the others that he was saved by a grizzly bear?

As I was thinking, another fiend attacked me from behind, first stalking up to my back, and then trying to sink his fangs into my large neck. He found me to be too big a mouthful, especially as I grabbed him by his neck with one hand, held him in front of me, and with the other hand removed his head from the rest of him. The black blood still spouted from his open neck as I tossed it away.

I saw one Indian with the right idea, grabbing a burning stick from what I guessed was a communal fire pit. He lunged forward with his new fiery weapon and torched one of the fanged fiends trying to make the Indian warrior his next meal. The fiend torched with such flourish that the warrior had to jump back. It burned like dry brush in a lightning storm. I must not have been the only one to observe the power of a fiery weapon, because other Indians grabbed up fire sticks. They started torching fanged fiends like dry brush.

The tide of war had definitely turned, and it was the fanged fiends going out with the tide.

The night was suddenly tortured by a scream from hell that not only rocked the world, but literally hurt the ears. Suddenly, all the fanged fiends of Jumlin turned and disappeared into the night. Taking their cue, I backed into the darkness of the night and morphed into my coyote form. I figured on tracking Jumlin's children and ending this by daylight. Only how does someone track ghosts? I found nothing to track, again.

I figured it was time to call it a night and head back to Dawn's encampment, but first I'd recon the area by air and see if I could find Jumlin's children. I might as well have looked for a ghost who did not want to be found. I did learn one thing this night: Jumlin's children might have been without their father, but they were not without a leader. When things turned against them, someone called a retreat, and they all instantly obeyed that call.

After the failure to find any signs of Jumlin's children, I made for Dawn's dark and lonely encampment.

Before joining her, I performed a recon of the area around the encampment and was surprised to discover somebody jawing with her. The personage looked familiar, buckskin outfit and all, but from above I could not make out who it was.

I continued my recon, just so I could figure out how I was going to land, dress, and not be spotted by Dawn's visitor. I finally came up with a plan: I'd change in flight into my silent-winged owl and would fly in from the opposite side of the wagon, land lightly, and dress quickly. Then I'd exit the wagon from the blind side and walk into camp from behind the wagon. My plan worked.

It worked so well, I almost got shot.

"Dam' Cody you must be part Indian," said a familiar voice.

If only Jim knew just how true that was!

"Sneaking up on me like that. Hell, boy, I almost shot you," Jim Baker exclaimed.

"Nice to see you too, Mr. Baker."

"Jim, just call me Jim."

"Okay, Jim. What has you sharing a trail with us?"

"Friends, and some strange scuttlebutt going around the forts of vampires in the area," Jim answered, looking straight at me.

"What, pray tell, are Vampires?"

"Some of the soldiers from the old country are telling about these nasty creatures of the night that attack people and rob their victims of blood by latching onto their neck and sucking them dry."

Remembering the fiend that latched on to my grizzly bear neck, I unconsciously started rubbing my neck feeling for puncture wounds.

"Something wrong with your neck, boy?" Jim interrupted.

"Not really, I just took a tumble out in the dark while performing my recon. I'm fine." I hope.

"As I was saying. Then those people killed by the vampire become vampires and kill more people. Hell, boy, there is one soldier who's telling folks he came to America just so he could sleep nights and not worry about becoming a creature of the night himself. Some Indians are speaking of a different creature that changes into a wild beast. These tales seem confused as to whether this other beast is a creature of good or evil. The Indians refuse to give a name to this creature, but again some of the soldiers have a name for it. In the old countries, such a nasty creature of the night is called a werewolf."

"Werewolf, what is a werewolf?"

"A creature of the night that's half-man, half-wolf and all beast. A werewolf is a man-eating creature of the night."

"Vampires, werewolves, no wonder so many of Americans come from overseas. You don't really believe in all these beasties?"

He pointed to the nearest artwork in the ground. "It's clear the Indians do. There are those soldiers from the old country that believe in this creature of the night. You asked if I do. I didn't totally believe the tales, until I came upon your missus here with her dirt drawings. I take it you have had a run-in with these creatures?"

I filled him in on the village of husks and that I had destroyed the village, infestation and all. I also told of the killing of the hunting party and the fiends we ran into there. I didn't tell him of the night's activities because I couldn't see how I could without going into too much Skin-walker information about me.

"Well, friends," Jim Baker said, looking at Dawn and me. "Daylight isn't too far off, so you two get some sleep, and if I get to nodding I'll wake one of you to relieve me. Don't be worrying about that. I haven't lived out here this long without knowing how to sleep with one eye open."

We took his advice and got some shut-eye.

Chapter Nineteen
~ Jim Baker ~

Come the morning, I woke to a wonderful smell, and the surprise of finding mountain man Jim Baker fixing breakfast. I didn't know what he was fixing, but it smelled so good my stomach responded.

"A good morning to you, youngster," Jim said, while Dawn looked on. Jim most likely would not have noticed, but Dawn looked a little unhappy, either at what Jim was fixing or that he superseded her duties of fixing breakfast.

"I'm just a fixing breakfast here. It's called appalos and is a secret recipe of us mountain men."

"I take it one of the main ingredients is strips of meat?" I said, for Dawn's sake. I wondered if I didn't say anything, when or if she would.

"You got that right," Jim answered.

"Dawn doesn't eat meat. Please don't mind if she doesn't have breakfast with us."

"Had a feeling something had crawled up her... Pardon, I mean ... I understand," Jim finally got out.

While consuming one great breakfast, Jim and I talked.

"I got to thinking last night, might be a good idea if you come with me today. I was fixing to visit one of my Cheyenne brother-in-laws and get his take on all this ... Jumlin's children. He ain't but a half day from here, and, if nothing else, you can make some friends. You could probably use some friends out here, traveling with a Navajo and all."

"Sounds like a good idea," I answered. I hoped it wasn't the village that was attacked last night.

After breaking camp, Jim and I took point together while Dawn followed with the wagon.

Nearing mid-afternoon from the position of the sun, we finally came to a distant village. Jim broke the silence that spying the distant village had created. "You and Dawn hang back while I go in and start introductions. When I fire one shot, come on in. If I fire more than one shot, pull up stakes, beaver out of here, and don't look back."

While Jim rode into the encampment, Dawn pulled the wagon up so she was sitting right next to me. We seemed to sit forever …

Eventually I became concerned. I got out my binoculars from their case and had a look. First thing that caught my sight was the skeletal remains of a number of tepees, burned down to blackened lodge poles. The second was Jim and some Indians having a very animated conversation. Jim pointed at something beside them. I moved my extended glass in that direction and discovered three hanging skeletons. Why would Indians hang skeleton remains of their own dead? Then, on closer investigation, I discovered the answer to my conundrum. These hanging skeletons had fangs. They were war trophies.

Moving the glass back to Jim and his associates, I discovered the conversation had ended and Jim was marching in the direction of his horse that some brave held for him. Jim did not look happy, but he didn't fire a shot or shots as any signal. I put the glass away and waited for his eventual return.

Jim came trotting out and didn't stop until he passed me. He turned his mount and came to roost just beside Horse and me. "Cody, all this talk of vampires and Jumlin's children… I really didn't believe it until I saw those fanged skeleton trophies hanging inside my brother-in-law's village."

"Yes, I know—" I started to interrupt.

Jim beat me to it. "Yes, I spotted the sun gleaming off your binocs there. My brother-in-law, Chief Red Wing, told an interesting tale. He said Jumlin's children tried to Indian up on the village last night, but luckily, for the village, Old Brave Bow sleeps very little and called out a warning to alert the village it was under attack. The warriors tried fighting them off with "hawks and spears." Seeing my confusion on the use of "hawks,' he clarified, "Hawks, tomahawks." He said it with a chopping motion with his hand.

"Yes, I know what a tomahawk is. You threw me with the short name," I said.

"Yes, well anyhow, the Chief said the hand-to-hand wasn't going well using the tomahawks." He emphasized the word 'tomahawk.' "The spears didn't hurt them either. He claims things changed for the better when he spied his totem animal majestically watching over the combatants from atop his tepee, a very large Golden Eagle. Just then, one of the braves grabbed up a burning stick from the night's fire and discovered these Jumlin's children torch like a bush of wild wheat during a drought. More braves, including the Chief, grabbed up burning sticks from the fire and so many of these creatures of the night lit right up. Then, on some god-awful scream, they all fled the field of battle. With all this upheaval and death in the village, this is not a good time for visitors."

Interesting, the Chief said nothing about help from a large grizzly bear.

"I'm family, and some were not happy with my presence, but my brother-in-law is the Chief. I'm going back to help with the dead and to watch in case of the possible return of these vampires. I suggest you continue on and get as much land between you and here while the light lasts." The last, he said looking right at me.

"One suggestion: rest by day and travel by night, keeping a burning torch in hand and one or two with the wagon. Travel slowly and carefully, watching for a possible vampire dry gulch and you might be able to make space between you and this tribe of vampires."

With that, we shook hands, and Jim Baker, the mountain man, and I went our separate trails.

We took Jim Baker's advice and turned away from the village and got the wiggle on to clear the area as fast as possible. The idea was not to clear the area of the possible second attack, but to save the village from that second attack by not being in the area. If Jumlin's children were looking for me, if they were somehow feeling my magical self, then maybe my absence from the area would save Jim Baker and the village from a second attack.

With that in mind, we laid as much trail dust between the village and me while we still had light. Come nightfall, we stopped to rest the horses and to make a campfire. We also made some torch sticks for the wagon. With my heightened eyesight, I didn't figure on needing a torch to see to travel. I was still debating if I should carry one to fight off a possible vampire ambush and chance Horse getting hurt by the closeness of the open flame, or not carrying one for Horse's greater safety.

After preparations were complete and the horses rested, I figured to continue on for the night and wait for the safety of sunrise to get some sleep. I shared my plans with Dawn.

"If you find yourself getting too tired to continue before sunrise, let loose a loud owl call to get my attention. It will be safer to stop early and set up a night camp with a large campfire than to allow someone to Indian up on you because you fall asleep on the wagon."

"What's this 'Indian up' you speak?"

"No offence: 'Indian up' means to sneak up on."

"I be fine."

"I'm sure you will be. Just remember my words."

With two torches set up and lit on the front of the wagon, attached near the bench seat sides but back far enough not to hinder Dawn's getting on or off the wagon, we continued our journey into the night.

Even though I could see just fine to continue traveling hard by night, I slowed our pace for the sake of Dawn and the wagon. Despite the night, we rode ahead.

Riding point, I kept a sharp eye out for Jumlin's children and the progress of the moon. Watching the moon helped me decide from time to time when I would call a break to rest the horses and also to see how Dawn was handling this all-nighter. As far as I could tell from break to break, she handled it just like the trooper she was. So we continued our journey through the night trouble-free so far.

I couldn't help but wonder why we hadn't been troubled by these Indian vampires. Was it possible they were back attacking Jim and his Indian family? I sincerely hoped not. Was it possible we had gotten ahead of them, and, they being on foot and Dawn and I with horse and wagon, were keeping ahead of them? Possible, but there was no way to tell. Well, there was one way that was tempting me, and if I was alone I very possibly might have at some point changed into Red Wing's totem animal, the Golden Eagle, and performed an aerial recon of the area and tried to spy them out. Leaving Dawn in the camp alone was just too dangerous for her and the horses right now.

When we came upon a sizable river, I led us up in the direction of the river, looking for some crossable point.

Come daybreak, I was just about to call it a day, when I noticed something disrupting the distant horizon. Halting, I removed my binocs and discovered a distant town looming over the far horizon. As I was putting away the binoculars, Dawn moved up beside me, wagon and all.

"Town up ahead. Possibly a good place to rest for the day, get some sleep, some food, and give the horses a good feed and rest."

"Hmmm," was Dawn's only response.

Maybe she was considering the possibility she might not be welcomed. Well, she was with me so dad-gamut she'd better be welcomed.

Coming closer to the town, things just didn't look right. Too quiet.

Chapter Twenty
~ Journey's End ~

Just outside of town, I found a sign that read Journey's End. The sign was full of holes, bullet holes! Looking straight down Main Street, I saw nothing. The street was empty of all life. No horses hitched to horse rails, no town folk about their business, no nothing. To all appearances, this was a real ghost town.

I caught a sign of movement. It was a dog or fox scurrying across an empty street. It stopped about halfway across, possibly because it had spied me. Just then, there was a screech from the sky. The animal ducked just as a large bird of prey swooped down and grabbed up the little vermin and flew off to enjoy its newly found lunch. I hoped witnessing the death of the town's possible last resident wasn't going to be bad medicine for Dawn and me. Bad medicine. Great! Now I was starting to sound like a damn Indian.

Dawn had hung back, so I gave the signal for forward and slowly rode into Journey's End. Wine, women, and song. Dust, dirt, and blood-sucking vampires look more like our future.

Riding into town ahead of Dawn and the wagon, I kept an eagle's eye out for any sign of life—movement from a window, the slightest sign of movement from a darkened doorway, anything. I was welcomed with silence, a real ghost town.

The whole town was a ruin that the prairie was claiming as its own. I could not help but wonder why. Most of Colorado's War of the States had been fought in other states. This could not be a dried up mining town because the mines were not that far off and were doing well. Indians, perhaps?

I saw the saloon with one of the batwing doors laying where it had fallen within the doorway of darkness, and the other hanging loosely and at a slant by one dried up hinge. Not very welcoming.

Across from the saloon was a brick building with caged windows, and if that wasn't enough to identify the building, over the doorway was a dried out Sheriff sign.

I moseyed Horse over to the calaboose, dismounted, and after tying Horse, I walked through the open, but not welcoming, doorway. Once my eyesight adjusted to the limited light coming in through the barred windows, I pretty much found what I expected: an unused disarray of decaying disuse. Out of mild curiosity, I checked the jail cells and found the barred accommodations in creaky, usable shape. I even found a key ring with keys to the working jail doors hanging on a nearby nail. It was not near enough to be reached from within a jail cell, I noted. In the back of the room was yet another doorway. Leading where?

On investigating, I found the rooming accommodations of the sheriff to be dusty and dirty, but possibly, in better shape than anything else we would probably find in this ghost town. Hearing from a horse other than Horse reminded me of Dawn, so I cut my investigations of the sheriff's abode short. Walking back through the jailhouse proper, I found Dawn still sitting in the wagon with the derelict saloon behind her.

I called out to her. "This place looks abandoned. Get down and have a look around while I take the horses over to that stable building down the street and see to their care. Be careful inside these buildings. If the insides are as rickety as the outsides, they could be dangerous. I would not suggest going up any stairways, so keep to the ground floor."

I moved Dawn's horse, wagon and all, toward the stable building, with the idea of leaving the wagon and supplies near it during our stay. Nearing where I had left Horse, I stopped long enough to untie him and then walked both horses to the stables.

Once there, I unhitched Dawn's horse from the wagon and led the two horses into the stable building. I had a look around and found the place usable, sunroof and all. Leaving the horses for a moment, I walked through the structure to have a quick inspection of the corral area. To my surprise, it was also in usable condition. Walking back to the horses, I unbridled Dawn's horse and gave him a pat on the romp that sent him running through the stable building and out the back into the corral.

After relieving Horse of his burdens, I walked with him out to the corral to see how the situation was about food and water. Looking around, I found the corral had enough wild grass to keep the horses fed, so the next question was water for them. I easily found the watering trough in the same condition as the rest of the town, in unused disarray. I bet the trough leaked and the water pump brought up dust and dirt.

I walked over and worked the pump and, to my pleasant surprise, water came forth. I was even more surprised when the watering trough failed to leak. The horses taken care of, I started looking for Dawn. At the same time, I was starting to feel the results of our all-nighter. Walking back through the stables, I made a point of fetching my long irons from their respective rifle scabbards.

Leaving the stables, I found Dawn standing outside a building that barely read Martha's Place over the doorway behind her.

"Ground floor rooms fine."

"Great, get your bedroll from the wagon, pick a room, and get some sleep. I'll grab my roll and get some shut-eye in back of the Sheriff's place." I started to head for the wagon when I turned back. "Any idea what might have happened here?"

"No," she answered in her terse typical style.

On entering the sheriff's office, I checked out the barred cells again. I even went so far as to check if the locks still worked, and they did. I was working on a plan, but for now, what was more important was getting some sleep.

A minute later and Dawn was waking me. I almost gave her a good one right in the chops. My military training was already getting rusty. Then I noticed the light in the room was different, and I smelled her veggie stew and warmed up bread.

"Sun down soon."

I'd slept the day away, and it only felt like a minute ago that I'd put my head down for a nap. Getting my boots on, I looked at Dawn. "Ever been in jail before?"

"No."

Moving over to the table to get at her veggie stew and bread, I glanced at her. "There's always a first time."

After wolfing down her dinner and grabbing some water from a canteen, I walked Dawn into the sheriff's outer office, and pointed at the open cell. "Get in."

When she looked a little confused. "We are running no more. Here I make my stand against Jumlin's children. Get in that jail cell."

Moving her in the right direction, I explained. "By day we're safe from these beasties. By night, you will be safe in there," I pointed into the jail cell. "Nice and locked up where those blood-sucking fiends can't get to you. While I face these beasties, you will be nice and safe, locked away behind iron bars, your own little impenetrable fortress."

Closing the cell door behind her, I fetched the door key from the wall nail. "Single-handedly I plan to use my best hit-n-run strike strategy with the help of my Skin-walking magic against Jumlin's children. You'll be locked away where they can't get to you, and where I don't have to worry about you!" What was coming next was objectionable, but necessary. I hoped she didn't see this as a lack of self-confidence and let it unnerve her. "Here, take the keys, just in case come morning I'm not able to let you out."

I saw the concerned look growing on her face as I handed her the keys through the bars. "Just in case, that's all. Remember, I'm not only the mighty magical Skin-walker, but I'm also the Captain of many a military engagement. I did better than survive. I learned military tactics from them."

I made a point of closing the sheriff's door as tight as possible. While there was still light, I rushed over to the horses and got them in for the night.

As the sun was calling it a day, I got busy setting up torches and lighting them around the town, not just for lighting up the streets, but also as weapons strategically placed. I also made a point of setting up caches of spears and bows and arrows around town, making sure the bows and arrows were near flaming torches.

When I figured the town was as prepared as possible for vampire guests, I ducked into a building near the sheriff's place, lost my clothes, and changed into the mighty Golden Eagle. I went on an airborne recon, first circling the town and then moving outward in ever-growing circles around the town, ever vigilantly looking for any sign of movement. I looked for any sign of Indians traveling by night, which would only be Jumlin's children.

Even a mighty magical Golden Eagle could not keep the aerial recon going all night long without refueling. When my moon shadow spooked a long-eared rabbit out of hiding, I figured it would be a mistake not to take a short dinner break, and I swooped down upon my frightened little dinner. Okay, so it took two attempts before I snagged my dinner, but I did snag it, and I made a quick meal of it. Getting back into the air, I was feeling a little guilty at having a nice juicy dinner while Dawn spent the night in a cell not knowing what, if anything was going on. How would she feel if she knew I was spending her jail time eating a nice juicy little rabbit?

With the guilt growing, I soared straight back to the town and had a fast, guilty, energetic recon of the town. I found…nothing. I even landed on the stable building to look in on the horses, and they were nice and quiet for the night. Surely, that was a positive sign that the area was clear of vampires. If a vampire was anywhere within miles, those horses would smell predators in the wind and would be moving about nervously in their stalls.

I flew by the hoosegow and released a mighty screech to let Dawn know I was about. Then I performed another circular aerial recon of the town and discovered I wasn't the only night flyer in the area. Flitting around between the buildings, I spied bats out looking for little morsels of dinner. How would bats react to vampires in the area? Would they even care?

Spreading my circular aerial recons outside the boundaries of the town, I started to see more and more wildlife activity in the area. This could be a good sign that the vampires where nowhere around, if the area was so busy with normal beasties. The more wildlife I saw, the more I doubted there were any vampire beasties in the area, and the hungrier I got. Remembering my last guilt trip over dinner, I just kept the aerial recon going as long as possible.

As the moon was getting ready to call it a night, I not only was getting hungry, I was getting thirsty as well. I swooped by a lake not far from town and spotted fish. Nice big bass or bass-like fish. Breakfast was served.

An internal voice spoke. What of those blood-sucking vampires? Not a single sign of any vampire beasties, none. That quieted my voices. I swooped in and grabbed me a big one right out of the lake. I dropped by the lake and grubbed down on my game meal. Dinner done, I cleaned my claws and beached to quench my thirst.

Back in the air, I swooped in toward town and performed one more complete recon of the town and the nearby area as the sun was rising. I swooped into town, landing just outside the building housing my clothes. I changed, dressed, and found Dawn eagerly awaiting her release from white man's prison walls. Walking by her jail cell, totally wagged out, I asked her to douse the torches and see to the care of the horses, trusting everything asked would be done. I went into what was now my bedroom and dropped into bed for the day.

What seemed like minutes later, Dawn woke me with the smell of meat. Seeing the surprised look on my face, she smiled.

"Made stew just for Capt. Cody. Veggie stew includes rabbit meat."

I quickly planted my feet into my boots and almost jumped to the table. While diving into the rabbit stew, I reached for a metal cup and was again surprised when I smelled...whiskey. I looked up at Dawn.

"Found bottle saloon. Hope good."

It was.

While I made quick work of dinner, enjoying my rabbit stew and whiskey, Dawn sat quiet. Near the end of dinner, she rose.

"I go jail, lock."

Finishing dinner, I walked into the sheriff's office proper and rattled Dawn's cell door to make sure it was locked tight. She just sat on the jail cell cot and watched. She was never one for a lot of useless words.

Leaving the sheriff's door shut tight, I made for the stables to check on the horses. I wasn't checking on Dawn's care of the horses. I just wanted to check on my best bud, Horse. Of course, he was fine and as glad to see me, as I was to see him. After I finished giving Horse some attention, I gave Dawn's horse a little muzzle rub and some soft words. Then I headed out to perform the real work for the night. First, I saw to getting all the torches lit for the night and gave my weapon caches a quick inventory.

With the sun starting to set behind the mountain off to the west, I went into the building next to the sheriff's building and lost my clothes and human form to become the mighty great Golden Eagle. As such, I went aloft to perform my aerial recons.

My first circular recons were the same as the night before. First around the town and then increasing my circular recons out away from the town. Everything appeared normal, with plenty of wildlife around and no signs of any human or human-like life to be found.

Following my second uneventful circular recon of the town, I was starting to feel hungry and took that as a sign that I needed to eat so I could continue my aerial recons. Wouldn't you know it, now that I needed some critter to volunteer to be dinner, I couldn't find any meals running around. Remembering last night's great fish dinner, I swooped in the direction of the lake.

One pass over the lake and I found my next meal. Swooping in for the catch, I came up with wet claws and no fish. I'd missed.

On my second attempt, I successfully grabbed up a nice large dinner. Dropping down next to the lake, I took the time to enjoy a nice fish dinner and some cool lake water. Then, I took to the air again, feeling nice and satisfied and ready for anything, and I got it.

I was nearing the town to start another systematic recon, when I heard a lot of squealing and flapping of many wings, and the dark sky got darker as a large swarm of bats fled the town!

As I neared, I heard banging and the sounds of terrified horses. They were the sounds of Horse and Dawn's horse. That's when it hit me. The lack of wildlife when I was looking for some dinner should have warned me.

Trouble had arrived.

Chapter Twenty-One
~ Attack of Vampires ~

Worried and again feeling guilty about my fish dinner, I swooped in over the stable building and circled the structure and found nothing. There was no sign of any movement around the stables or any of the nearby structures. Inside the stables, both horses were banging their stall doors, wanting out, wanting to get clear of something that spooked them. From a hole in the stable roof, I looked in and found nothing amiss inside the stables. I was tempted to give Horse some soft words of encouragement, but that would require a physical change and I wasn't sure I had the time for that. Something was spooking these horses. If there wasn't anything near the stables, there was something in the wind, something fairly close.

Taking flight, I flew over the hoosegow, still finding no signs of activity. For Dawn's comfort, I sounded off with a mighty Golden Eagle screech, to let her know I was nearby and on the job.

I performed an aerial recon of the town and found nothing amiss, except for a deadly quiet. Not even a cricket was to be heard. Raising my superior hearing to the max, I failed to hear the slightest sound of a single insect scurrying about. This silence was creepy. The only sounds were the wind going past my head and the panic of the horses.

Starting my second circle of the town, I neared the point where Dawn and I had first entered. I spotted a cloud of dust in the distance. I came to roost on the first building I had passed on entering the town and watched the distant cloud slowly come closer. I took some time studying it because something didn't look right. As I watched, I realized what seemed so strange about this cloud. It wasn't strong enough to be created by an army of horses.

As I watched, it hit me; it had to be an army on foot. The way animals like horses act and react around these demons, they couldn't possibly have horses. They'd have to be on foot.

Before I went out to meet them, I figured it would be a wise idea to see if what was in front of me was all of them or if a separate contingent of these demons was coming from another direction.

So I performed one more aerial recon around the edge of the town, checking for any signs of another group approaching the town from a different direction. I saw none, but it was interesting to note just how empty the area had become of any wildlife anywhere. It was as if all wildlife in the area had just left. All wildlife, that is, except the horses and one lone Golden Eagle.

The town appeared to be secured from all directions except the one where Dawn and I had entered. I started to swoop over in the direction of the oncoming demonic dust cloud. I was sure it had to be none other than Jumlin's children finally arriving. Flying to meet the enemy was not easy. I had to fight a strong impulse to fly away. All my Golden Eagle survival instincts screamed to fly in some other direction, any other direction than the one toward which I was flying. Hearing the scared sounds of the horses, and remembering Dawn all locked up alone, depending on me and trusting in me, helped my human instincts to keep command and fight off nature's very powerful survival instincts.

My human mind in control of my eagle self, I flew straight toward them and over them. An unnumbered army of these creatures from hell just kept marching toward the town. They appeared like an army of grey-skinned redskins, typically half-clad in buckskin britches or with only a buckskin cloth around their midsection.

Strangely, none appeared to have any weapons at hand. I saw no spear, bow and quiver of arrows, and not a single tomahawk in their midst. I continued to fly around them and discovered something even stranger. Not one of these demons had looked upward at me, not one. They all kept marching toward the town as if I was not flying right over their heads.

I continued circling them for a while. Not once did I see a single demonic Indian look my way. Eventually, this gave me an idea.

I flew back to town and changed into my wolf-man form. Ignoring my hairy nudity, I started pulling down wood off the decaying buildings and, after building a pile, used one of the torches to start a large bonfire right at the entrance to town. I built the pile as a little mass in the center of the street by plan.

Using a flaming torch nearby, I set a board on fire and tossed it onto the center of the pile, lighting it from the center outward. I watched it ignite, and as the fire rose, I wished to change back to my Golden eagle physique, and I went aloft fighting all eagle natural instincts. I carefully swooped close enough to the fire to grab up a large piece of burning lumber from the non-burning end and took flight. This wasn't easy. All my senses told me I could burn myself. Eventually I started feeling like I was burning myself, and I had to look down to make sure I wasn't.

I flew right over the demonic army and dropped the burning lumber onto them. About four or five of these vampire redskins started screaming. They torched easier than the dried out lumber I had dropped on them. Others failed to stop their progress in time, and even more of these vampire demons began screaming. They torched themselves from accidental contact with the original torched demons. The rest separated from the burning ones and ignored them. They kept marching toward the town.

I flew back to town to watch their approach from my perch on the building at the beginning of the town. I watched as the demonic dust cloud kept coming closer. I was tempted to grab up more burning lumber and continue dropping it on them like bombs, but it was against my Golden Eagle nature to continue with that tactic.

The demonic army of vampires kept coming.

As the army neared the fire pile, I moved into position two: From street level a block behind the fire pile, I dropped onto the street while changing into wolf-man form. In position, I grabbed up a bow and quiver of arrows from a pre-arranged weapons cache stored next to a flaming torch.

The fire pile created a slim point of entry for the enemy to enter. As they passed that pile, I shot fire arrows into the deadly dry vampire bodies, watching them torch into screaming zombies of fire. After enough of them had torched, that entryway was totally blocked by an elongated pile of fire.

Eventually, I couldn't tell where the original fire pile and the pile of flamed vampires started and ended. Both flaming piles had joined to become one burning, impregnable roadblock. The damage was greater than planned. The pile of burning vampires stretched close enough to the building on the right side that the building started burning.

That entryway was completely impassible.

The next move was up to the vampire army. Would they enter the town from the next street, one block to the right? I figured the left was out of the question. Left of town was the river we had followed that led us to this town. Was it possible I had convinced them to leave town altogether, at least for the night?

I turned back into my mighty Golden Eagle form and took flight to aerial recon the demonic army's next move.

They moved, almost as one, to the right and started up the next street. At least this street took them away from the horses and Dawn. Two blocks within the town, it also was totally blocked by a building that had collapsed into the street.

By the time they discovered their folly, I had landed on the roof of a building across from the downed building, right next to a flaming torch and cache of weapons. After changing into my wolf-man form, I lifted the ladder that permitted either Dawn or me to light or put out this rooftop torch. Then, I grabbed up a bow and an arrow and, after igniting the point of the arrow, let fly the flaming projectile, igniting me some vampire redskin. Before that fiend was torched, I was already preparing another flaming projectile, with the goal of igniting me another vampire Indian.

In such close, confused quarters, I only had to ignite a few bloodsuckers, turning them into screaming, mini-piles of flame, and the flames spread to those around them, further igniting them. I was enjoying the screaming mayhem and getting total enjoyment from the growing glow of the flames, as more and more of the fiends bumped into others, igniting even more of themselves.

The pleasure of the moment came to an abrupt end when a loud, god-awful scream came from somewhere outside of town. The vampire army turned and marched out of town to disappear into the darkness,

Was the attack ended for the night? Was this night's fight over?

Still in wolf-man form, I ran to the edge of the building and judged the distance. I jumped from rooftop to a slightly lower rooftop and then ran to the edge of that roof to watch the further retreat of the army of vampire redskins. After they were well gone and out of sight, I had to deal with another worry.

Rushing to the roof edge nearest the burning building, I checked out my newest concern: Will this building start a chain reaction of burning buildings? Would my fiery blockade burn out of control until the whole town burned down?

I wasn't concerned for the town per se. I was worried about what we'd do without the guerilla warfare benefits the town was bestowing on us. I was worried what we would do if we had to face that demonic vampire tribe out in the open.

To my relief, I could see from the burning glow of the building that it shared no walls with any other buildings, and with the wind blowing outbound from the town, it looked like there was a good chance this building would burn down without igniting any others.

From my vantage point, I kept an eye on the fire and watched for the possible return of the army of vampire redskins. An army now about two-thirds diminished and properly routed by one lone werewolf.

After a while, I considered changing into Golden Eagle form and performing an aerial recon around the town, just in case the vampire tribe was regrouping for another attack from another direction. Then it occurred to me the horses had settled down. It had been a while since I had heard from them. As I was considering this a good sign, nature provided me with another comforting sign. The bats were returning. Apparently, the bats felt it safe enough to return to their town to rest out the daylight.

Feeling good about myself, I realized I might be one lone werewolf, but I was one mighty lone werewolf.

As I watched over the town, eventually the moon went to bed and the sun greeted a new day with its vampire-preventing rise of golden radiance. The sun also awakened the sounds of nature around the town, which in turn awakened a ravenous appetite in me.

All seemed well, for now.

With the area safe from attack, I changed into my Golden Eagle figure and plunged off the building, wings wide. I swooped by the hoosegow and announced myself and my intentions with a mighty screech and flew off to get me a nice meaty breakfast or more.

Eventually, after getting my fill of nice meaty morsels, I returned to town with the goal of getting some well-needed sleep. As I neared the stables and the building next door that housed my clothes and personals, it occurred to me that I had a bit of a problem. What if Dawn was out and about? I couldn't very well drop from the sky and switch into my naked human self to enter the building to get dressed with Dawn standing right there where she could possibly see me naked.

I made a point of circling the area first before landing, looking for any sign of Dawn being about. I didn't see her. By now, she must have been out of her nightly impenetrable fortress and inside some building where she would not see me land and change. So, I landed, gave the area an eagle eye and, still not seeing Dawn, switched back into my human self and hurried into the building to dress.

Walking out into the light, my heart almost stopped.

"That was quite a performance there, young whippersnapper."

Chapter Twenty-Two
~ The Town ~

"In all my years, I'd thought I'd seen everything, but an eagle-man?" Coming out of the deep shadows between two buildings, an old miner, from his clothes, emerged pulling a mule that looked like it had seen better days. Reflexively, I started to reach for my side iron I had just finished adjusting on my hip.

"Don't shoot," the old man called out. "Maulie and I aren't no owl-hoots."

I tried to regain my composure after this new development. "Maulie?"

Dropping one hand, he pointed behind him with the other. "Maulie, my mule." He dropped the hand holding the mule's reins. "She and I have done a lotta livin' and seen a lot of strange things, but we never seen no eagle-man before. Damnedest thing, seein' a big old eagle land and turn into a plum naked man. I'd heard some strange tales from the local redskins over the years, but none about no eagle-man."

Seeing his gaze change direction, I also looked toward the hoosegow from which Dawn was approaching us.

Had she hidden from this miner? If so, good.

"Navajo," the old man announced. "That there's a Navajo squaw." He looked at me. "You have a Navajo female with you? In these parts?"

"Dawn, my traveling companion," I said as an introduction.

Shaking his head, the old man stared at me. "An eagle-man and a Navajo." Scratching his head, he suddenly slapped dust off his hat. "You're a Skin-walker?"

As the sheriff's room had about the only chairs and table in usable shape, we continued our palaver in the sheriff's back room.

138

Dawn put out some grub for a nooner as I told my tale of how I came to be a Skin-walker, and how we came to be in what was left of this town now under siege.

"You sound like someone to ride the river with, youngster. Taking on five owl-hoots for two Indians, with whom you haven't smoked a peace pipe. This old 'skin healed you with this ointment that changed you?" He sounded doubtful.

"That's right. You saw me change from a Golden Eagle."

"I did that, I did."

"You've come to a dangerous area for mining, old man." I figured it was time to warn him of the dangers of the area. "As I said, I spent the night warring with a large tribe of vampire Indians, and I figure on their return tonight."

"Yep, I knows of those … vampires you called them. Didn't have a name for them myself. I've just been keeping a scarce of them for years. 'Specially seeing what they did to this town and all."

That piqued my interest. "You know what happened here?"

"Yep. Used ta chaffer here in town, then tangle foot myself into this calaboose here. Told them vampire Indian ups on the town."

It took me a moment to realize he'd said that he used to do business here, then whiskey up, and get thrown in the jail. "So what happened to this town, old man?"

"Well, some psalm singer with a passel of pilgrims decided this here was their new holy land and put up in this here town. The trading post and the saloon were quite fancied a might by the local ground diggers in the area. Wasn't long before people started waking in the mornings feeling a bit off, some complaining of feeling drained. Town's people went from feeling drained to feeling weak and sickly. Eventually, people started dying in their sleep.

"The psalm singer tried to make medicine to clean the evil out of this here place. He called it a … ex-or-seism or somethin' like that. …Things just worsened. When the psalm singer failed to wake one morning, all his pilgrims kind of got to figuring it was time to pack up and get gone."

"This was a religious town, led by a man of the Bible, and it had a saloon?"

"Back then there was a passel of mining going on not far from here. Those ground diggers would come to town to supply up. Guess someone wasn't against making some wampum off the ground diggers by selling them some firewater. Might take note of the hoosegow placed right across the street from here many a ground digger saw the inside of this here building. Town made wampum on that, too."

"You're saying the town levied fines on those who broke the law?"

"Don't know 'levied,' but if a jailbird wanted to fly back to his mining, he had to pay through the nose to get out. I should know, place cost me a-plenty, it did." He momentarily smiled at old memories.

I interrupted. "How do you know what sickened this town?"

"You seen that one building all torn down?"

"The one that blocks the street with its damage?"

"That was the psalm singer's place. Had a cross on top of its bell tower and all. After the pilgrims left this town, that one building, and only that one building, was torn down to the ground. Most of the rest of town has been slowly taken back by the prairie.

"Don't nobody mine this area no more 'cept Maulie and me. Too many miners go into those hills and don't ever come out."

"If it's so dangerous, how is it you still mine this area?"

"Learned to stay out of them critters' way, I have. I also have Maulie. If'n she gets restless we get the wiggle on. If'n she wants to get the wiggle on, we make beaver in any direction she wants. She's been keeping distance between those owl-hoots and us for many a year."

Thinking about how Horse acted when the vampires got anywhere near, it made sense. All this jawing and feed bagging after a night on the warpath was catching up with me. I was feeling a real need for some sleep.

"I figure this vampire tribe will be back on the warpath again tonight. I suggest you put Maulie in the stables with the horses and, come nightfall you lock yourself up with Dawn for the night while I do battle with them tribal blood-suckers."

"You must be one mighty Skin-walker to be taking on a whole army of those blood-sucking critters."

I was tempted to ask him how he knew of Skin-walkers, but I was really feeling dragged out. That conversation would just have to wait for another time.

"Four years commanding soldiers and planning wartime strategies gives me something of an edge. Johnny Reb's taught me a thing or two about guerrilla warfare. That's come to be useful."

"Well, all that may be so, but I'd be happy to be far from here come nightfall. Believe Maulie and I will be making beaver out of here and just leave you to your little war."

"Best to you, old timer," I said in way of a good-bye.

"Same to you, young whippersnapper. Same to you."

Last I saw of him, he was heading out of town in the opposite direction from which the tribal vampires had attacked the night before, and opposite the direction from which they retreated. He led his good luck charm behind him.

I started to look in on the horses and discovered Dawn was already at it. As tired as I was, I was mighty happy to let her do it. I went to get some well-needed sleep.

Round two of the lone werewolf versus the Vampire Tribe was only hours away.

Chapter Twenty-Three
~ Round Two ~

As always, Dawn's wake-up came all too soon. I made quick work of some leftover stew from earlier. As I walked out to the street, I noticed Dawn was already caged for the night. I judged there was enough sun for me to look in on Horse, so I did.

As always, Horse was as glad to see me, as I was to see him. "Just stay calm tonight. I'll do my best to keep those blood-suckers from getting anywhere near you." With that in mind, I gave him one last muzzle rub, and rushed out of the stables.

I moved next door and relieved myself of my human possessions and then my human form, changing into my wolf-man form. My first duty was to get the strategically located torches aflame. Next, I rebuilt the lumber pile at the end of Main Street, only this time I built it long enough to close off the whole street, and then set the pile aflame from the last torch I had set to flame for the night.

The plan was to move the fight away from Dawn and the horses and move it up another street. Considering what had happened the night before, I was concerned whether they would go up the next street. I sure hoped so. I had weapon caches that hadn't been used yet.

With the sun setting for the night, I shifted into Golden Eagle form and went aloft to perform an aerial recon of the town, ever enlarging my circular recon to include the surrounding area. I figured one side of the town was safe from attack because of the river. I doubted these tribal vampires would attack from the direction that the old man had taken. That still left a large area from which the vampires could come. Nothing said they had to come from the same direction as the night before, and nothing said they had to come from the direction to which they had retreated, either.

On my third circle of the town, I heard the horses getting restless, not banging in fear like the night before just before the attack, but they were definitely getting restless. Maybe they sensed trouble coming, or I flew by too low and my mighty predator form spooked them.

On my next pass, I gave the outer perimeter my strongest eagle eye and realized the wildlife in the area had gone quiet or into hiding. First the horses, now this. Was trouble in the wind?

Then it happened. My survival instincts screamed fly away, danger. My humanity just barely kept control of my mind and wings.

I made yet another circle of the town and still saw nothing of the enemy. The survival urge to leave the area grew stronger. I decided during the next pass to come to roost on a tall building across the street from the building I had used the night before, the building next to the burned out building. This gave me a good view of any possible approach to the town from a wide angle.

From a block behind me, I heard the horses getting more restless, including the occasional bang of a stall door. One or both horses were getting restless enough to test the strength and integrity of their stall doors. While most of the town was in ruins, the stable building, with the exception of part of the roof, was in fairly good shape and strong enough to hold the horses for as long as needed, I hoped.

My survival instincts kept screaming, "fly away."

I just kept telling myself, Dawn and the horses can't fly away. Who was it who totaled two-thirds of the tribe of terror? Who was it who was going to take out the remaining third? ME. That's who.

A chill on my back reminded me how nice Texas was this time of year. Fine, after we wipe out this army of vampires once and for all, we'll go to Texas to winter. That didn't calm my Eagle instincts for self-preservation as much as I had hoped it would.

Off to the right where there were some trees, I thought I saw movement. Darker movement within darkness.

I trained my eagle eyes in the direction of those trees and watched and watched.

I saw movement as four figures darted out from the trees and headed straight for town.

Grabbing up two spears with my claws, I decided to take the fight to them. Plunging off the roof, I swooped down in their direction. With the spears sideways in my claws, I dove on them, bowling them to the earth. Once I hit the ground, I quickly changed into my wolf-man appearance and grabbed up one of the spears. I picked up and moved the spear into a defensive position just in time to have one member of the vampire tribe charge into me and impale himself with a scream.

Snapping the spear in half, I knifed the smaller part of the spear right into the chest of the second vampire as its charge followed the first. His eyes rolled up as his body dropped in front of me.

I started to move for the second spear at my feet, but the third vampire was on me too quick. As his arms reached for my neck, I grabbed for his shoulder and moved backwards, letting his momentum send him flying and rolling over and beyond me.

As I got to my feet, the fourth vampire was already on me. Long-fingered hands locked low on my neck, preparing to sink his fangs in my neck. He positioned his fangs in just above his vise-like hold on me. I changed into my larger grizzly bear form and foiled his plans long enough for me to pull him off like the leech he was. I enjoyed ripping this foul creature's head off.

The other foul creature I had tossed over and away from me came crawling up my back. He reached my shoulder and prepared to sink his fangs into me. I grabbed him, pulling him off me like pulling off a lake leech. I brought him around to the front of me and ripped his head off, tossing both his head and his body away from me before any of that foul fluid spouting from his neck should attack the fur of my grizzly bear personage.

Hearing distant growls, I discovered six more vampires charging my way. I quickly changed back into my Golden Eagle form and flew back to town. As expected, the pack of Indian vampires followed.

Coming to rest next to a flaming torch and a cache of weapons, I grabbed up a bow and some arrows and started flaming the points. I let them fly, but missed more than I hit with my rapid-fire tactic. They kept coming. One arrow that was going to miss brushed under an outstretched arm as it passed and ignited the vampire's arm.

I watched as he stopped to put out the fire, but the flame quickly stretched over him like a plague, totally engulfing him in seconds. These creatures were highly flammable. The rest just kept coming.

I kept up my onslaught of fire arrows until I suddenly realized I was out of arrows and still had one vampire coming for me. Grabbing up a large, mean-looking tomahawk, I jumped off the roof onto a porch cover, and from the porch cover to the ground. The lone vampire just kept coming.

As it got closer, I stood my ground. When the vampire could almost get his elongated fingers around my neck, I slipped sideways and plunged the tomahawk deep into his shoulder, so deep that his shoulder was nearly dismembered from the rest of him. In shock, the Indian vampire screamed in pure pain and turned to escape. I almost jumped him to finish him off, when I had a better idea.

Changing to my Golden Eagle physique, I flew to the roof holding the weapons cache and grabbed the last two spears from the depleted cache. Weapons gathered in my claws, I flew after the injured Indian vampire still in retreat.

Once I reached him, I had to circle him like a buzzard. His progress was slowing. As I circled, he struggled forward with great effort. My predator self was unobserved. Eventually, he collapsed, not reaching his goal.

He had been making for a mountain ridge, but the blood loss won the race. I landed next to him, and changing into my wolf-man form, I reached down and ripped off his head and tossed it away just to make sure he was dead. Unlike his predecessors, with their open necks spouting foul fluid, very little blood leaked from this one's open neck.

Having a good look around, I discovered a darker area within the side of the mountain. I'd found a cave entrance. Picking up the spears, I made for that entrance. Once there, it was obvious that if I still had my normal night vision, I wouldn't see my hand before my face, but with my Skin-walker enhanced night vision, I saw quite well.

From the entrance, the cave moved inward about ten to twenty feet and then moved to the right. I entered.

When I reached the turn to the right, two vampires jumped me from nowhere. Both went for my throat. One succeeded in knocking the spears out of my hand, disarming me proper. The sudden attack rendered the spears useless because they attacked so suddenly.

Changing to grizzly bear made my neck harder to reach or penetrate. I grabbed the first one and, yanked it off me like pulling off a lake leech. I ripped off its head and tossed it away.

The second vampire had latched onto me from behind, and, when I reached for it, the vampire Indian quickly dodged beyond my reach.

When I tried grasping it from my other side, it was still too far to reach. Worse yet, it tried to bite into my back instead of going for my throat.

Letting out a frustrated roar, I slammed backwards into the cave side, successfully smashing the vampire leech off my back. I quickly turned, found the dazed little humanoid leech, and ripped off its head. I then froze, listening for any signs of additional guards on the approach. There were none to hear.

Changing back to wolf-man form, I retrieved the dropped spears. Taking the turn within the cave sent me straight on with a slightly downward turn. I continued on, ever vigilant for the sounds of additional guards. I met none. Eventually, I emerged in a circular room large enough for my Golden Eagle presence to soar. I saw no need for that at present ...

In front of me, on a large stone throne sat a human-like form about twice my size. He appeared to be as muscular as he was tall. He began to lose his human-like appearance from the neck up. His fiery red eyes stood out in this darkness and almost appeared inflamed. Below his very pointed nose was a pair of fangs that would have made great daggers in length and apparent sharpness. If this wasn't enough to declare him 'not human,' there were the horns protruding from his bald scalp. At first, I thought his feet were hoofed, but a second look proved that he had unusually fat feet with pig-like toes.

I would have been happy to have ended my observations there, but I could not help noticing he was totally naked. A protrusion coming from his lap looked like it would more likely rip a woman open than impregnate her. He sat on his throne like he was made for it and it was made for him. Beside his throne, four members of the vampire brotherhood stood, two on each side. Could this foul creature be Jumlin himself?

Before I could ask, his guards attacked.

The first one came at me with such a rush that I raised my spear, expecting him to impale himself on it, but just as he got within range of the spear, he pulled up and tried to slap the spear away. Thinking fast, I dodged by bringing the spear under his swinging arm and brought it back up, lunging forward to pierce his evil heart.

Before I could bring the other spear into play, the other three were all over me. Their combined weight was enough to tip my balance and bring me down.

With a mighty roar of defiance, I altered my appearance from wolf-man to the mightier grizzly bear, making it more difficult for these fiends to put the bite on my thicker hide.

In my fury, I pulled the one on my chest up to my face and crushed its head with my mighty jaws. The putrid fluid that discharged into my mouth was almost enough to cause me to pass out. I wouldn't do that again!

Tossing the dead weight off me, I was regained my footing with the other two still clinging to me. Grabbing at the next one, I tried to pull him from me, but he had entwined his elongated fingers into my fur enough to make detaching him a problem. Instead, I grabbed his head in both of my powerful paws and crushed it until it imploded, with his eyes exploding into the room.

That left one vampire, and it was going for my eyes. I grabbed this foul creature by the upper arms and pulled both of its foul appendages outward, to free it from my personage. I yanked outward with such force that both its arms tore free at the same time. With its arms in both of my hands, the creature dropped screaming to its death, while making a foul mess on the floor before me.

Tossing the arms away, I assumed my wolf-man nature.

Before me, the mightiest of vampire fiends sat on his throne with his eyes blazing brighter. I suspected I had pissed it off.

It spoke in a growling, grinding tone that could only come from hell itself. "You won the day, Skin-walker. I know what you are. My father spoke of such human servants of hell."

"Who is it that I'm about to kill next? Please, before I send you back to the hell where you belong, are you Jumlin himself?"

"No," he answered in a laughing, mocking tone. "Before you sits his first spawn."

First spawn, not first-born. Interesting.

"My all-powerful demon father was tricked and killed by a mighty tribe of warriors many moons ago, too many for me to recall. My father and I raped and robbed many a virgin squaw to form this army you squashed in nights of battle. You are truly a mighty Skin-walker, and you have won this day. In time I will create a new and mightier army, and some day, when age has robbed you of your might, I will return for you, mighty Skin-walker, and I will make you pay for this day."

That said he exploded into a large number of bats, each larger and blacker then the township bats, all with his blazing eyes and murderous fangs. I had no idea how to fight off so many attackers. They flew past me and over me in such a way as to pummel me in their passing, though none really did any damage to me.

I quickly turned and ran out of the cave with the idea of becoming my Golden Eagle personage and following after these bats. Come the morning light, I would pull this foul creature from hell out of hiding and introduce him to his fiery fate with the rising of the sun.

Outside the cave, all was quiet and peaceful. I could neither see nor hear any sign of the presence of the bats. I quickly looked in the direction of the town, with the fearful thought that Jumlin's spawn might start rebuilding his new army using Dawn, but all appeared quiet over the town.

Not too quiet, either, as I realize the sounds of nature was returning, a true sign that Jumlin's spawn was no longer in the area, and that Jumlin's spawn was no longer a threat.

Despite the signs provided by nature, I became the Golden Eagle and performed an aerial recon of the town and surrounding area before I would or could believe this vampire war was over. Flying over the stables, I took notice that all was quiet within, and even Horse felt the peace and quiet of the battle won.

Chapter Twenty-Four
~ The Aftermath ~

With a return to peace, I figured it was time for this predator to take advantage of the return of nature to the area and find some well-deserved and needed meaty sustenance. During my last fly by the calaboose, I sounded off to let Dawn know I was still in the area and still well. Now for that well-deserved dinner, or two, or three, depending on how good hunting was. With the sounds of peace in the area, I figured hunting would be just fine.

With the rising of the sun and a plentiful breakfast, I landed before the building, which held my human belongings, reformed back into Cody O'Conner, and ducked quickly into the building to take care of my too natural condition. In other words, I quickly got dressed. Coming out of the building and getting my holster properly placed on my side, I grinned at the pleasure of not being surprised like the morning before by that old miner.

I was torn between seeing to the horses and seeing to Dawn and providing her with my good news that the vampire war was, temporarily, at least, won and over with. I was thinking that after a couple of quiet days of rest, it would be a good idea to pack up, pull out, and head to Texas for some restful normality and to winter down south. Maybe I could find a town needing a sheriff, a deputy, or a rancher needing someone to break horses for him. Right now, I needed to tell Dawn the good news and start getting me some well-earned rest.

* * * *

As usual, I most likely was asleep before my head hit the pillow and the next thing I knew, Dawn was waking me, but this time I woke feeling fully rested and ready to face the day.

"You sleep two days. Time you get up," Dawn ordered in her typical stern way.

I got up, but I was not in the mood for biscuits or veggie stew. I went hunting for my breakfast enjoying the freedom of the hunt and the carefree feeling of not having to worry about doing battle with vampire Indians come nightfall.

When I wasn't hunting, the majority of the day was spent preparing to move out and head south. I took Horse for a ride for the fun of it, but mostly to get him some real exercise outside of the stable stall and the corral. Come night, I did me some hunting for dinner and brought back some critters to be skinned and salted down for the trip south.

The next day, with the wagon loaded and ready to go, we said good-bye to the old town by giving it our backs and heading for Texas.

Pleasant nightmares

Notes

Appalos

An early camp food made by skewering alternate pieces of lean meat and fat on a sharpened stick and roasting over a low fire. When it was possible to get them, pieces of potato or vegetable were intermixed with the fat and the meat. This method of cooking was often used by many tribes of Indians, as well as the Mountain Men.

> —*A Glossary of American Mountain Men Terms, Words & Expressions,* Compiled by Walt Hayward & Brad McDade

Denver City (a.k.a. Denver, Colorado)

Early records of Denver City, Colorado, later to become Denver, Colorado when the territories gained statehood, did have a Sheriff Pollock. Records show that eventually, Sheriff Pollock quit as Denver City's sheriff after the town elders refused to build a jailhouse, deciding a courthouse and republic house was more important. Since the city didn't have a jail, Sheriff Pollock would lock up prisoners in rooms at the hotel Sheriff Pollock personally owned and operated. Sheriff Pollock also quit due to city funding problems that made it harder for Sheriff Pollock to get his fee of $.50 per prisoner per night stay at his hotel from the city elders.

General George Armstrong Custer

On July 12, 1867, General George Armstrong Custer and seven companies of the U.S. 7th Cavalry arrived for duty at Fort Wallace. Fort Wallace saw so much Indian action that the fort gained the reputation as "The most Flightiest Fort in the West!" It was while stationed at Fort Wallace that the General Custer fought his first Indian fight, just miles from the fort.

The incident with the capture of Custer's wife is total fiction. Late in 1867, General Custer did leave Fort Wallace to visit his wife, whom he had left at Fort Riley. At Fort Riley, General Custer was taken prisoner and court marshaled for leaving his post at Fort Wallace. Some believed his court martial really had to do with his brutal handling of deserters.

Grizzly Bears
Grizzly bears are six to seven feet tall. My mystical magic Skin-walker grizzly is about two feet taller when standing up right.

Jim Baker, Mountain Man
Jim Baker was a friend and traveling companion to such names as Mitch Bouyer and Kit Carson. This very colorful mountain man had, in his time, married six times, all to Indian squaws. It's said that one of his wives was a Cherokee chief's daughter.

While the above is historic fact, his brother-in-law, Red Wings is an invention of the writer for the story's sake.

Jumlin, Legends of
They are Native American legends of Jumlin, the first Native American vampire, and the creation of his vampire children as described in the story.

Most legends don't describe his death or even if he ever died. Those legends that include his death only say he died by the hands of a mighty tribe of warriors. I created the death by spear and beheading for the sake of the story. The amulets to ward off Jumlin's children are also a creation of mine based on the idea of the cross warding off European vampires. By the way, some believe Jumlin's children not only existed, but still exist today. For more on the Native American Vampire look for *Vampire Owner's Manual*.

Kit Carson
For the sake of the story, I extended Kit Carson's military career by a couple of years. In 1867, Kit Carson's military career was honorably over, and he could be found at his retirement ranch in Oklahoma. He was making plans to go to Washington the following year to fight for Indian rights. In May of 1869, Kit Carson died of health issues.

Kidder Massacre
In June 1867, Lt. Lyman Kidder and ten men from the seventh Calvary of Fort Wallace started from Fort Sedgwick, Colorado, with messages for Lt. Col. George Custer, who was camped at the forks of the Republican River near where Benkelman, Nebraska is today. Custer, in the meantime had left for Ft. Sedgwick. Kidder, missing Custer's trail, assumed Custer had headed to Fort Wallace. When the Kidder party reached Beaver Creek in present day Sherman County on July 1, 1867, they were attacked by Indians, and no one survived. Custer sent out a search party when he realized what had happened, and on July 11, ten days after the massacre, the search party discovered the murdered bodies of Kidder and his men. None could be readily identified except for the Indian scout. From *Life at Fort Wallace*, internet site.

Mitch Bouyer
Mitch Bouyer, son of Sioux mother and French-Canadian father, is historically reported to be the best guide in the county, next to Jim Bridger. As General Custer's lead scout, Mitch Bouyer was killed at the Battle of Little Big Horn.

Nooner
Considering contemporary slang has redefined "nooner' as a lunch time or afternoon sex fling, thanks to the show Married with Children, I felt a note is required. Long before the above mentioned show, even as far back as the days of the Wild West, a "nooner' was a noon break for a midday meal. In some societies, the "nooner' was the most important meal of the day.

Owl as Death Bringer

Many Indian cultures believe the Owl is a Bringer of Death or a herald of death's coming. Owls are superior night predators, possibly because, unlike most birds, their flight is ominously quiet. This gives the owl a similarity to ghosts and the hush of ghostly movement. Some Native American tribes believe the owl has a close relation with ghosts.

Red Cloud, Greatest Sioux Chief
Leader of the Sioux, Red Cloud joined the forces of the Sioux tribes and the Cheyenne tribes and made war on the U.S. Army over what Red Cloud saw as the Army's encroachment on sacred hunting grounds. The war lasted from June 1866 to November 1868. During this time, Red Cloud led a campaign that included the killing of 81 officers and is known historically as the Fettermen Massacre, after Capt. Fettermen, who was leading the detachment.

Roadrunner
Roadrunners are so fast they can and do prey on rattlesnakes. The roadrunner will swallow down as much of the snake as possible, but can't swallow down the whole thing at once. So the roadrunner will indeed walk around for some time with the undigested part of the snake hanging from its mouth until it finally digests the whole snake at a rate of a couple of inches at a time. It depends on how long the snake is as to how long this process takes. As one who grew up as a kid watching Looney Tune Roadrunner cartoons, don't you think it was about time the coyote got the roadrunner?

About the Author

Timothy (Tim) Forder was born and raised in Maryland, USA. It's my mother's theory that I get my love of horror and fantasy from being born just a couple of blocks from the gravesite of Edgar Allen Poe in Baltimore!

I'm a very happy family man with a family consisting of a beautiful wife, a creative teenage daughter, (live-in) sister-in-law, Seeing Eye Dog and daughter's rabbit.

For some years now, I have been losing what little eyesight I have left to RP (Retinitis Pigmentosa). If you need someone to talk to about coping with vision loss or Seeing Eye Dogs feel free to e-mail me at Facebook.

I have been a huge fan of the horror and fantasy genre, specially the older material, since my pre-teen years. I was introduced to the genre by the family sitter. Sue and I had an agreement: If I didn't beat up on my sister I could watch Creature Feature with her, which was past my bedtime and after my sister went to bed. I will never forget Sue Greenspan's words of wisdom: "Remember, what you see in the movies is only make believe and can't hurt you." Years later, I was the man when my buddies and I would go see Hammer Horror movies at the local theatre, and I would sit in my seat laughing at my friends as they tried to take cover from the horror on the screen! Sue Greenspan, if you are reading this thank you for many fun filled hours with my monsters!

Started my college studies in Wildlife Biology. I wrote a thesis on Dracula that was picked as the year's best work. I was given the honor of reading the thesis to the class, and by sundown, the paper was both famous and infamous around campus! As a result, on campus my nickname of "Tex" (because of my flare for western hats) became "The Vampire".

A bookworm from my early years, I still consume books like food, only being blind, most of my books are compliments of The Congressional Talking Book program (books on special cassettes or the newer digital books for the visually handicapped).